THE LYON'S PUZZLE

The Lyon's Den Connected World

Sandra Sookoo

ARE YOU SIGNED UP FOR DRAGONBLADE'S BLOG?

You'll get the latest news and information on exclusive giveaways, exclusive excerpts, coming releases, sales, free books, cover reveals and more.

Check out our complete list of authors, too!

No spam, no junk. That's a promise!

Sign Up Here

www.dragonbladepublishing.com

Dearest Reader;

Thank you for your support of a small press. At Dragonblade Publishing, we strive to bring you the highest quality Historical Romance from some of the best authors in the business. Without your support, there is no 'us', so we sincerely hope you adore these stories and find some new favorite authors along the way.

Happy Reading!

CEO, Dragonblade Publishing

Additional Dragonblade books by Author Sandra Sookoo

Willful Winterbournes Series
Romancing Miss Quill (Book 1)
Pursuing Mr. Mattingly (Book 2)
Courting Lady Yeardly (Book 3)
Teasing Miss Atherby (Book 4)

The Storme Brother Series
The Soul of a Storme (Book 1)
The Heart of a Storme (Book 2)
The Look of a Storme (Book 3)
A Storme's Christmas Legacy
A Storme's First Noelle
The Sting of a Storme (Book 4)
The Touch of a Storme (Book 5)
The Fury of a Storme (Book 6)
Much Ado About a Storme (in the *A Duke in Winter* anthology)

The Lyon's Den Series
The Lyon's Puzzle

Other Lyon's Den Books

Dedication

To Amy O'Neal. Thank you for loving my books and for your support. Thanks also for being my champion when things are hard. It means so much.

CHAPTER ONE

October 10, 1817
The Lyon's Den
London, England

MONTAGUE BASSAGE, EARL of Pennington, sat back in his chair at the card table and kept his face schooled in his typical mask of boredom. Best not give too much away regarding his hand. Good or bad, his opponents didn't need a tell, for he adored whist, and rarely did he lose. Neither did he cheat; he simply had a finely-honed skill—or perhaps talent—for varying vices.

It was all part and parcel of the persona he'd created, a way to protect himself after fate had landed him two devastating blows.

But now, despite the enjoyment he derived from attending the high-stakes entertainments found within this particular gaming hell, he was bored.

Bored and disgruntled.

Bored, disgruntled, and tired. Of everything.

He glanced once more at the cards he held and wished the other men at the table would get on with it.

Bored, disgruntled, tired, and randy as hell if he were honest with himself. So much so that he stifled the urge to blow out a breath.

When was the last time he'd taken a woman into his bed? For that matter, when was the last time he'd availed himself of one of the courtesans available at the Lyon's Den? Each one was more beautiful than the last, and he'd known more than a few over the years he'd been coming to this establishment.

Damn, it had been a couple of months, surely.

Yet not even that bevy of skilled, perfumed women with silky skin and clouds of hair could lift him out of the pool of boredom he'd fallen into. He simply hadn't wished to put forth the effort of choosing one, of going through the effort merely for a quick rut in the sheets.

Yes, the physical release was something he would forever crave; he was a man, after all, but as he grew older such things weren't something he held at the top of his lists of interests. Of course, the only other option was to marry, engage in a romance with a respectable woman, and *that* was something he could never do.

Would never do, for he'd hidden his heart behind walls of steel and stone. Thus far, no woman had been able to find her way around it, and that was how it would remain until he popped off this mortal coil.

Love. Bah! It was nothing more than a fragile, fleeting phenomenon that broke a man down to his soul, made him weak, stole away every hope and dream, then tossed him back out on the streets to pick up the pieces of his life.

Never again would he be that man.

"For Jove's sake, Pennington, stop woolgathering and attend the game," the man on his right groused, for obviously they'd been waiting on him. The other three players had already revealed their hands to mixed results.

"Right. My apologies." Wishing to end the game and move on to new entertainment, Montague laid down his final trick—eight cards in the same suit including the trump card all in spades. "I believe this means I have won. Again."

Cards were no longer a challenge.

One of the representatives that worked for the Lyon's Den tallied up the winnings and divisions. At the end of the evening, the men could collect their winnings—or pay the house—once they saw the Abacas Woman.

"Damn it, Pennington, must you win every hand?" another player at the table complained as the men scrambled to their feet.

Montague shrugged. "If you don't like it, then study the game, Fulton. Improve your showing." He met the gazes of the other man and then the dealer. "If you will excuse me? I'm promised elsewhere."

Not quite ready to leave the gaming hell just yet, he wandered about the main gambling floor, glanced upward into the ladies' observation gallery, nodded at a few of them, ignored the sloe-eyed glances that might make a lesser man pelt upstairs, and then made his way into the gentleman's smoking room. The thought of imbibing rich foods nearly turned his stomach, and craving brandy, he went directly into the gentleman's lounge. Surprise wound through his chest, for the first man he laid eyes on was his best friend, Thomas—Viscount Ashbury.

"Ashbury!" Immediately, his spirits lifted, but not by much. "Glad to see you here tonight." The viscount was his opposite in every way, which is probably what had made them such fast friends since Oxford. Tall, broad of shoulder, and blond, Ashbury had always been outgoing and sociable. He sprinkled his charm about, and he was seemingly never bedeviled with doubts or dark thoughts.

Unlike me.

The other man's eyes lit, and he offered a wide grin. "Pennington! I hoped you might make an appearance eventually." They shook hands. "Care for a drink?"

"Absolutely." He followed the viscount over to an ornately carved sideboard where crystal decanters of the finest wines and spirits rested.

The owner of the Lyon's Den spared no expense in an effort to attract the wealthiest men of London.

And to take their coin. He couldn't prove it—no one could—but he suspected the Black Widow of Whitehall, Mrs. Bessie Dove-Lyon, the proprietor—rigged the games in her favor, because of course the house would always take a substantial cut.

"Why are you here, Pennington? You are exuding ennui and gloom." Ashbury pressed a cut-crystal tumbler into Montague's hand. The two fingers of brandy inside the vessel were a welcome sight.

"Where else would I be?"

Ashbury snorted. "At Pennington House, I presume. That bastion of darkness, angst, and sorrow. Where the heavy drapes remain over the windows and you keep yourself locked in your library, refusing to have visitors. Hell, half your staff is frightened of you."

"As it should be. I am not a good man." Over the years, he'd cultivated and collected vices as if they were expensive jewels. He drank to excess on occasion, held court with a bevy of different courtesans, gambled fortunes away—but then always made them back—and held a wicked temper. Every so often, he would indulge in blackmail, especially if a member of the *haute ton* conducted himself in an unseemly fashion. And, even more rarely, he'd indulged in a duel or two. His marksmanship was impeccable, and he'd called men out for trifling reasons.

In this way ensuring he was well and truly left alone.

"Gammon. You are, deep down when you aren't trying to convince yourself that you were meant to be alone." The viscount brought his glass to his lips and sipped. "When you aren't nursing heartache."

Montague grunted. He drained half his tumbler before answering. "The pain reminds me of why I cannot invite romance into my life again." Then he downed the remainder of the contents in his glass. "I don't mind being alone."

For long moments, Ashbury stared at him with speculation in his eyes. "Do you want my opinion?"

"No, but you will give it regardless."

"True." The viscount drained his glass, winced as he swallowed. "I think you *do* mind being alone, which is another reason why you've shut yourself away."

"Bah." He waved a hand in dismissal as a few more men entered the lounge. It was becoming rather crowded in the room. "You alone know why I've done that." When the other man would have spoken, Montague shook his head. "Worry not, my friend. The largest issue besetting me currently is boredom. Nothing holds my interest. There is nothing new under the sun."

"Perhaps." Ashbury rested his glass on a nearby table, and when Montague did the same, he led the way out of the room. "But that just means you need stimulation, on more than a few fronts. Why not indulge with one of the courtesans upstairs? I'm certain you favor one or two."

"I do, of course, but I've had enough of them to fill a ship's hold." Was that a good or bad thing? Depended on perspective, no doubt. He huffed, fell into step with his friend as they entered the private gaming room. "There is nothing new in that bevy of flesh either."

"Perhaps if you would venture out from your usual willowy brunettes?"

"I doubt that." He shot his friend a look. "I have no interest in women. Too much effort."

Did it make him deranged? His past two fiancées were indeed slender with flowing brown hair. He hadn't sought them out because of that; it had merely happened. The fact that he only bedded courtesans of the same looks was beside the point.

Or it wasn't, but he didn't wish to delve too deeply into the state of his mind for fear he would be found mad indeed.

"How do you know if you don't try?" Ashbury waggled his golden eyebrows. "No wonder you are bored. A man needs variety in everything—including bed partners."

The words rankled, for he'd often wondered if he wasn't doing himself a disservice by limiting his trysts like that. "Can I help it if I enjoy perfection?"

"Bedding women of the same type is *not* perfection, my friend. It's falling into a rut. If it was, you would have wed all of them." Ashbury cast him a glance filled with empathy. "Bedding women who have the same basic looks as your previous fiancées won't bring them back, Montague," he said in a whispered voice.

Some of his reserve began to crack around the edges, and that made him uncomfortable. As well as remember. Those feelings rose within his chest, but he tamped them back down as best he could. Now was not the time to lose himself to grief.

Again.

"I know that." The words were forced from a throat tight with emotions. "Yet in a way, it makes their losses not quite so acute."

Ashbury moved into his sightline. "I would believe you, except you are not moving away from those events in your past, Pennington. You are dwelling on them, letting them fester to a point that you are infected by memories and are constantly looking to recreate them. You are being eaten alive as if from a cancer."

"I cannot help what I am, Thomas." Montague shoved a hand through his hair. "If not wishing to let go of those memories or wanting to lock myself away behind closed drapes in the dark makes me a beast, I shall gladly take up that mantle, for there is nothing else for me in this life."

He had found love twice, but fate had yanked it away, and he rather doubted he was strong enough to go through the same a third time.

"It's a sticky wicket." The viscount heaved a sigh and settled his gaze on two men who were ingesting bottles of brandy one after another for the entertainment of a ring of other men. No doubt wagers had been proffered to see which man would pass out first. "However, you need an heir. You are getting old, my friend. There is no more time to dance about the issue or pamper your softer feelings. It's time to marry."

Perish the thought.

Montague grimaced. He wished for a glass of whatever liquor was handy. "That may be so." For too many years, he'd quite forgotten the need to have an heir, probably more sooner than later. At the age of two and forty, there was no guarantee he would last for another decade on this earth. "I'm loath to do so."

"Why?"

"I cannot give away my heart again, just don't have that in me any longer." He pinched the bridge of his nose. "Most of me died three years ago." When he'd lost his second fiancée to the machinations of the criminal element while she was out shopping with a friend. Two years before that, fate took his first fiancée due to a fever. "I simply cannot—won't—put myself into that position. Not any longer."

"Of course. I understand that." Ashbury clapped a hand to Montague's shoulder. A cheer went up from the ring of men, for one of the drinkers had collapsed onto the thick Oriental carpet. "Some would say you don't have a heart regardless."

Amusement tugged at the corners of his mouth, but he didn't quite grin. "The tittle-tattle is quite correct. A man wracked with grief and steeped in vices can no longer have a functioning heart, and that is as it should be." With a glance at the ring of men, he strode over to the sideboard that was no less lush than what was in the gentleman's lounge. Would that he could dive into a bottle and stay there indefinitely.

Honestly, he just didn't care about anything in his life.

Ashbury accepted the tumbler of brandy Montague handed him. "Perhaps you should consider asking Mrs. Dove-Lyon to match you."

He choked on his next sip and spent the next several seconds sorting himself. "And what? Wed a woman steeped in scandal?" What kind of life would that be? "Neither of us needs that." It would take a tremendous undertaking to land them both back into society's good graces, for the women Mrs. Dove-Lyon matched to wealthy men as well as peers were often bent and bruised from scandal and gossip.

"As if you aren't touched at times with scandal?"

"I didn't say I wasn't, but that is who I am. I won't apologize for it."

"Perhaps a woman in the same circumstance won't either. Doesn't that say something for her character?"

"Do shut up, Ashbury." Montague drained his glass and winced against the bite of the liquor in his throat.

His damned friend snickered. "Aren't you tired of merely existing in your dreary townhouse, alone, with only your staff as company?"

"Not particularly." He transferred his attention to a different knot of men. Heaven knew what the hell they wagered on this time. "I have my books, my brandy, and my cat." To say nothing of his paintings, but that was a well-guarded secret. Not even the viscount knew of *that* particular talent.

"Satan?" Ashbury laughed out loud. "As if he makes your eclectic tendencies better?"

Montague grinned. "He is a black cat and just as big a curmudgeon as me. We are well suited, and there is no better companion." Except when he stuck his damned whiskered face where it wasn't needed. Time and time again the feline had come away with paint on his fur or had nearly set himself on fire by passing too close to a candle.

And, the best thing about him was that cats didn't break his heart. Satan always regarded him with barely tolerated disdain, which was how he liked it.

"There is no hope for you, Pennington." The viscount shook his head as he sipped at his drink. "This is why I worry."

"You needn't. I've survived this long."

"Not survived. Existed. Called defeat. There is a difference, and it's appalling."

Montague didn't deign to answer. He moved to one of the card tables in the room—faro this time—and took one of the vacant seats. Ashbury did the same. For one moment, all eyes went to one of the high-ranking representatives who worked directly beneath Mrs. Dove-Lyon, for he often circulated through the rooms to keep an eye on the guests within. Mr. Vance wasn't easy on the eyes, but he had sharp business acumen and a sharper wit. He made certain to toss out men in dun territory or with pockets to let, and the occasional man who mistreated the courtesans.

Then normal activity resumed.

The dealer at the table, dressed in black, glanced at him. "It's a fifty thousand pound buy-in, Lord Pennington."

Mr. Vance raised a dark eyebrow and crossed his massive arms at his chest.

Well, Montague didn't particularly care for the blatant display of force or security for the establishment, he recognized that it was needed. "Easily covered. My account is already on file with the Lyon's Den." He glanced around the table at the three other men. Two he didn't recognize, but the third he did as Barton Kentwood.

As the game of faro began, he kept up a steady stream of conversation with Ashbury. Truly, they both could play this in their sleep, had made a tidy income with it during their university days. Card after card was presented and bets placed. Wager after wager fell, and Montague won each. Ashbury groused half-heartedly, but the baron's face blanched. Truly, the man had no skill in this.

By the time the deck was exhausted and another dozen wagers were placed, Montague had increased his initial deposit by four.

"I apologize, Lord Pennington, but I am unable to cover this loss," Lord Kentwood said as he tugged on the knot of his cravat. "However," he held up a hand, palm outward when Mr. Vance came forward, "I *can* offer you the hand of my youngest daughter. She is nineteen, and in need of a husband. I'd rather have her off my hands in any event. Save on the Come Out, you see."

What the devil is this, then?

"I…" Montague narrowed his eyes at the baron. The last thing he wanted was a wife, and a young one barely out of finishing school at that.

Ashbury nudged him in the ribs with an elbow. "Might as well take her. Put a babe in her belly and then send her off to your estate in Essex if you find you cannot stomach a wife."

His chest tightened. *I don't want a wife.* Slowly, he shook his head. "I cannot do much with your chit of a daughter, Kentwood. I'd rather have your coin."

A red flush rose over the baron's collar. "I haven't the funds, you see. Barely enough to enter the game…"

Mr. Vance approached the table. "Shall I escort him out, Lord Pennington, or shall I go upstairs and ask Mrs. Dove-Lyon's opinion?"

"Perhaps that would be best." After all, she was the owner of the gaming hell. And he rather doubted she wished to be cheated out of her cut. "I will wait." Montague stared at the baron while Mr. Vance left the room. "I'm sure you understand."

"Of course, of course, but you wouldn't be sorry with my girl, Your Lordship." His face was visibly sweaty. "She's a real looker. Loads of chestnut hair and big brown eyes."

Well, damn. "I'm certain she is quite lovely, but I am not in the market for a wife."

Eventually, the towering Mr. Vance returned. At the table, he bowed from the waist. "Mrs. Dove-Lyon has determined the hand of Lord Kentwood's daughter is as valid as coin." When Montague groaned and Ashbury chuckled, the man continued. "She also said that if you lose the next hand, Lord Pennington, she will sort the arrangements immediately, so you don't renege on the agreement. After all, a young woman's life and future is now in play."

"And if I win the next hand?" he asked around clenched teeth.

Mr. Vance offered a small grin. "Then you shall have the choice on when *you* wish to wed Miss Stapleton."

I am right properly stuck. "Fine." Montague glanced at Ashbury, who shrugged. He was confident of his skill at the table, but he ceased to care any longer about anything else. If he were forced into marrying, so be it. The cold facts were that he *did* have need of an heir. After that was accomplished, he would have more freedom to perhaps drink himself into oblivion and leave this sorry life.

To land in a place where he could toss emotions and memories behind and could stop hiding them. Let them rip him apart.

Mr. Vance cleared his throat. He gestured to the dealer. "You may proceed with the next game, if you please."

"Of course, Mr. Vance."

"Also, Lord Pennington, that means you must offer another fifty thousand pounds to proceed."

Montague gave a terse nod. The stakes were always high at the Lyon's Den but this one felt quite excessive.

The dealer scooped up the cards left on the table, shuffled the deck, and then dealt another hand to those men who were still playing.

Mr. Vance tapped the baron on the shoulder. "Lord Kentwood, if you will please come with me? Mrs. Dove-Lyon would like a word."

I'm sure she would. Montague snorted. No one escaped the gaming hell without scratches and scars, but he was determined to beat the owner at her own game.

The baron's face blanched again, and he left the room with the larger man.

By the time wagers were placed on the first few turns of the cards, a small crowd had gathered about the table. Apparently, word had gotten out. No doubt men in the crowd were wagering even now on the outcome of this game.

Nerves beset Montague, for the hand he held was uncommonly terrible, but he wasn't skilled in cards for nothing, and he proceeded to bluff his way through the next few turns. Annoyance lanced through his chest in a hot wave, for with every subsequent turn, he grew further away from the hope of winning.

How was the dealer doing it? He narrowed his gaze on the man in the black, but there was nothing amiss he could see. Now more than ever he was convinced there was mischief and possibly cheating afoot, for he never had such a terrible hand before.

By the end of the game, he'd lost horribly, never even had more than three cards in the same suit. Wretched luck or orders from the owner? And adding insult to injury was the fact that he'd lost to Ashbury, who sat there chuckling as if it were all the greatest folly he'd ever seen.

"Bah!" Irritated beyond measure, Montague threw his cards upon the table and pushed back his chair with such force it crashed into the man standing behind him. "I grow weary of this tonight. If you will excuse me?"

Then Mr. Vance was there, like a giant, looming specter. "Lord Pennington, if you will come with me? There are contracts you'll need to sign in Mrs. Dove-Lyon's presence, and terms to discuss with Lord Kentwood."

Bloody, bloody hell.

The last thing he wanted to do was wed, and to a young miss to boot. But there was truly nothing he could do. All wagers and results were final here at the Lyon's Den. He refused to offer up his heart in this forced union, and if the chit couldn't survive his monstrous temper—in fact it brewed and grew even now—then that wasn't his problem.

Everyone in London knew he was a beast.

CHAPTER TWO

October 12, 1817
London, England

WIDOW ADRIANA ROBERTS née Stapleton frowned as her younger sister Sybil continued to argue with their mother. This had been going on for the last hour, and quite frankly, a megrim was beginning to brew because of it.

"Why would you make me do this, Mama?" Sybil was her junior by fourteen years and had been a surprise baby for her parents when they'd assumed they were much too old for such things. Yet she was the youngest of the family and easily the most beautiful. Tall and willowy with ethereal looks as well as hair the color of a doe's skin. She would have made a brilliant match…

…until Papa had lost a hand of faro, couldn't pay, and had no other choice but to offer Sybil's hand to the worst man in London.

As if they were still living in the Middle Ages instead of the nineteenth century.

Their mother wrung her hands together, the perfect picture of female helpless befuddlement. At the last second, Adriana tamped the urge to roll her eyes. "Your father is in dun territory, Sybil. There is only so much he can do."

"How does that affect me?" Sybil frowned, for apparently in her nineteen-year-old world, if society didn't revolve around her, she couldn't comprehend an idea or situation.

Merciful heavens.

Adriana huffed in frustration. Surely her sister wouldn't go on being a beauty without the brains. "Papa's pockets are to let, or to put it into rather bolder terms, we are near bankruptcy. That means you *have* to marry Lord Pennington." She shrugged. "At least you will be a countess, so it's not that large of a sacrifice. Hasn't Mama always wished for you to marry well?"

Nothing less than a title for her baby sister. Hot jealousy speared through her. Men had always been interested in Sybil, even while she was still a schoolgirl, while Adriana had struggled for notice, and when one man—*not* with a title—had shown a glimmer of notice, her parents had pounced, and that had been that. She'd been married off, to save the expense of having a spinster on their hands.

Wed to a right proper bounder.

That she may or may not have murdered.

Not that the truth mattered, for scandal had followed and her reputation had been shredded beyond recognition. The fact that she'd moved back home with the family caused ongoing tension and concern, for she might damage Sybil's precious chances for an advantageous match.

And yet, here they were, in a bind because of their father's inability to ignore his vices.

"That's not *fair!*" The whine in her sister's voice grated across Adriana's ears.

"While I agree he's not an ideal match, at least you will have security and a title. That is more than most women can hope for in this life." Truly, the world wasn't kind to women—unattached or otherwise—and if one didn't have money of their own, even more so.

Sybil frowned, but even in a snit, she was almost transcendent. When Adriana frowned, her round face tended toward a double chin and the gesture made her seem vastly unapproachable. Or so she'd been told, multiple times by her mother. "But Lord Pennington has so many vices!"

"Men usually do." Though, to give her sister credit, Pennington's *were* rather vast.

Gambling.

Drinking.

Carousing.

Probably lying, and by all accounts a beastly sort of lord.

"Perhaps you can change him with your goodness," Adriana said in an offhanded manner. She was merely glad it wasn't her slated to wed *that man* in two days, as the contract her mother held indicated. Marrying one reprobate had been quite enough.

Their father was suspiciously absent from this meeting.

The coward.

"But, Lord Pennington is just so... so... old!" The wail echoed through the drawing room. Tears welled in Sybil's brown eyes—the only physical feature they shared. "I have been cheated out of *everything*!" Of course she would choose to emphasize that word. She implored their mother with a watery glance. "Why shouldn't Adriana pay the price for Papa's sins? She's the scandalous one, the Stapleton daughter who has rumors attached to her name. In that, she would be Lord Pennington's perfect match."

The words were like hot, sharp knives thrust into Adriana's chest. "Why, because we are both on the edges of society? We both are trailing gossip and tittle-tattle that no one ever wishes to verify?" She couldn't quite keep the bitterness from her voice. No one knew the reasons behind the scandal that held the black cloud over her head, for she'd kept that horrible secret to spare her parents as well as her sister.

And yet no one appreciated the discretion or the sacrifices she'd endured in her ill-fated marriage.

Before their mother could interject, Sybil shrugged. She dabbed her eyes with a dainty, lace-edged handkerchief. "You had your chance, and now it's gone, but I will *never* have one! No Season! No courtship! No envy of my friends with how many handsome men I can bring up to scratch!" The silly, vain girl dissolved once more into tears. "I *really* wanted a duke." A sob swallowed up that last word.

"So did I," their mother commiserated, with tears in her own eyes.

Oh, bother.

No one had said boo about Adriana's marriage to a no-account merchant, and no one had ever thought that she could have landed a man with a title, for she was too petite, too pleasantly plump—that was the kindest of descriptions she'd heard about herself—on the shelf too long, and too prone to plain-speaking, which had branded her difficult.

Now she was all but forgotten, unless the old rumors from three years before resurfaced for whatever reason. After all, the *beau monde* did love to cut others down.

Adriana pointed her gaze to the ceiling. True, Sybil was meant for better things than marriage to such a horrid man, yet she needn't act so privileged and spoiled. But the more she pondered the issue, the more an idea began to percolate in her brain. No one should have to bear the pain of a wretched husband; she well knew the strength needed to survive, and truly, since she'd already gone through that gauntlet, it *should* be her to fulfill Papa's debt.

"What am I going to do, Mama?" Sybil wailed and cried into her handkerchief.

"You must buck up, dear, and do what is necessary." Their mother wrapped her arms around the distraught girl. "At least we shall receive a small but tidy income each year upon your anniversary. Pennington agreed to that."

Then, of course, Sybil would be lauded in the family as the one who saved the Stapletons from the poorhouse, and once more, Adriana's history would be forgotten.

For once, I would like someone—anyone—to be proud of me.

It was a rather silly wish for a widowed woman of three and thirty whose life had already been ruined and consigned to rumor.

As her tortured thoughts turned, Adriana briefly held her bottom lip between her teeth. Sybil was correct, though. She'd already had her life, her one chance at happiness. It hadn't worked out, so what was one more sacrifice? It would be her last gift to her family, for if the rumors swirling about Lord Pennington were true, she probably wouldn't survive a month with the tortured lord.

"Never fear, baby sister," she said in a choked whisper. "I'm certain something will come to light that will spare you from such a life."

If fate were kind, those words would come to pass.

October 13, 1817
The Lyon's Den
Whitehall

KNOTS OF WORRY pulled in Adriana's stomach as she alighted from a hired hackney cab on Cleveland Row. Would she be granted access to what was rumored to be one of the most unique and notorious gaming hells in London? That remained to be seen. She frowned as she contemplated the light blue, four-story building with attic rooms on top. Truly, it was a rather unassuming edifice on an otherwise boring street.

Was she in the correct place?

Pulling a scrap of paper from her reticule, she peered at the address hastily scribbled on it in the darkness of midnight. After talking with her father—he was halfway into his cups so probably wouldn't remember the conversation—she'd ascertained the location of the place where he'd gambled away Sybil's future. He'd babbled on about a woman called the Black Widow of Whitehall, and from the bits Adriana had been able to ascertain before he'd hurried from the house for his club, that particular woman was the owner of said establishment.

If anyone could help her, it would be she.

Yes, this *was* the place. As she took a deep breath and let it ease out, she stuffed the scrap of paper back into her reticule. Illumination shone at nearly all the windows, so obviously the house contained life of some sort. There was no sense in further delay. Best have the errand out and done with so she could return home, and hopefully without being missed.

Ironic, that. She smirked as she approached an unassuming door on the right side of the building's front. It wasn't as if her reputation could become any more stained than it already was. If this were truly a gaming hell of unique origin that let both men and women enter, no doubt the women were funneled through the smaller entry point, for no matter how progressive the proprietress might be, women were still considered the lesser sex and generally had not the same rights as men.

And men would always be seen as superior.

Bastards, all of them.

The second she reached the door, it swung inwardly open to reveal a woman of indeterminate years clad in a black gown, dark hair pulled tidily back in a plain bun.

"How can I help you?" Her dark gaze glittered in the dim illumination as she looked Adriana up and down. "I rather suspect you are not here to indulge in gaming."

"I am not, and even if I had the means, I would never. Throwing one's hard-earned coin away on naught but chance and fate seems irresponsible."

"Then perhaps you are here to apply for a courtesan position?" Again, the woman looked her up and down.

Heat smacked her cheeks. "Good heavens, no. That is a worse vice than gambling." She didn't care if her plain speaking wasn't well-received; that was simply how she felt after watching her father's fall from grace.

The trace of a smile curved the other woman's lips. "Then why are you here?"

"I wish to request an audience with Mrs. Dove-Lyon." When the woman in black's eyes widened, she rushed onward. "It is a matter of some import."

Slowly, she nodded. "Very well." When she stood aside, Adriana passed into the building. "My name is Helena. Who shall I say is calling?"

"Adriana Roberts, formerly Stapleton. Eldest daughter of Baron Kentwood."

"I see." The door closed behind them. Helena gestured to a door on the left. "Please wait in the ladies' parlor while I ascertain whether Mrs. Dove-Lyon is in residence tonight."

"Thank you." As her heartbeat raced and the knots of worry made themselves known once more in her belly, Adriana wandered into the parlor.

From deep in the interior of the building, sounds of revelry and laughter arrived muffled to her ears. Luxurious furnishings met her eyes, the carpets plush, the drapes velvet, the upholstery shot with gold thread. From first appearances, owning a gaming establishment was quite a lucrative business.

There was no more time to wonder, for a door on the opposite side of the room opened, and Helena was there, beckoning to her.

"Mrs. Dove-Lyon is most anxious to see you." She led the way through a series of rooms where other women milled about. Then they entered a servants' passage, no doubt to navigate the halls more quickly and without detection. After they ascended a set of wooden stairs, Helena led the way out of the passage and into a proper corridor. A blue-painted door waited at the end of the short hall, and it was at this panel that Helena paused. "She is waiting for you, and her time is limited as well as quite valuable." Then she pressed the shiny brass handle and pushed open the door. "I shall wait here to guide you back out."

"Thank you." Though she didn't fully understand the need for secrecy nor the implied cloak and dagger actions, Adriana's muscles were tight while she entered the spacious apartment. However, since the lamps burned low and were in the places most likely to provide strategic, mysterious shadows, she couldn't readily determine the colors of the décor.

Nor could she easily discern anyone else in the room with her, but she knew someone was, for the faint rustle of fabric gave away her presence.

"Please, make yourself comfortable Mrs. Roberts."

She frowned, for she would have preferred to see the owner of the bold, confident voice but quickly sank onto a low sofa and folded her hands in her lap. Glad that her cloak hadn't been taken upon entry, for it covered the gown she wore that was a few years out of date. "Are you Mrs. Dove-Lyon?"

"I am." Again, fabric rustled. Movement in the room alerted her to the presence of the other woman, but the heavy shadows persistently clung, and when the Black Widow seated herself in a chair across a furniture grouping from Adriana's location, the only part of the woman she could see halfway clearly was her lap and legs. Everything else was lost to the bizarre lighting. "And you are the eldest daughter of Lord Kentwood." The conversational tone was no doubt designed to draw her into a sense of comradery or relaxation.

But Adriana didn't have any reason to trust this woman. "Yes."

"I have heard about you, Mrs. Roberts. There are rumors surrounding your name saying you killed your husband."

Heat again slapped at Adriana's cheeks. Even in this she couldn't escape her past. "I cannot help what the gossips will say. I only know what my truth is."

"Mmhmm. I do enjoy a woman trailing scandal. They always make for the best stories." For long moments the other woman remained quiet. "Your life during that marriage wasn't the best it could have been." It wasn't a question.

"That is correct."

"No children resulted of that marriage?"

"Also correct." An ache set up around her heart, for it was but one disappointment she must always carry. There had been that hope, once upon a time, but her husband had made certain it was never fulfilled. Subsequent years had seen her all too barren.

Perhaps that had been for the best, for if he had been horrid to her, he would have also been the same to any children they might have had.

"Ah." For long moments, the Widow of Whitehall remained silent. "Your life after Mr. Roberts's death hasn't been an easy one."

"Of course not. With my father nearing bankruptcy with each breath and the scandal that has followed me which prevents me from obtaining a position within a proper household, I have faltered." She didn't know why she admitted any of this to the other woman. "Creditors took everything I owned—" well almost everything—"and forced me to move in with my family."

"Thankfully they took you back even with a younger, more viable sister at home."

Another round of heat suffused Adriana's cheeks. "Just because a woman is well past the first and second blooms of youth does not mean she is worthless, Mrs. Dove-Lyon." If her tone was more clipped than she intended, so be it. She had grown rather tired of being overlooked and dismissed due to age.

"You have no family of your own. That will not endear you to marriage-minded men, for they will assume the worst," the widow continued, as if she had gotten to this sticking point and couldn't move past it.

When her chin trembled and quick tears stung the backs of her eyelids, she tamped down the emotion as best she could. "Given the circumstances I lived through, perhaps fate was kind in that regard." This woman didn't need to know every aspect of her marriage.

"Interesting." Another swath of silence followed while Adriana pleated a section of her skirting. "You still possess quite the spirit."

What an odd observation. "Why shouldn't I? Life has been difficult, but that doesn't mean I should have turned over and given up, waiting for the grave."

"No, I don't suppose it does." Fabric rustled as the widow shifted position. "I met with your father two nights past."

"I am aware of that, and the outcome of that meeting is why I am here right now." Her hands shook so badly that she clasped them together.

"Oh? It is not my policy to discuss anything that happens within these walls." She drummed her fingers upon a knee. "Especially to outsiders."

"While I understand that, I feel this *is* a matter of some importance. You see," Adriana leaned forward, but the shadows in the room were difficult to penetrate. She couldn't clearly see the woman's face or her form. "My father couldn't cover his gaming debts, so he offered Lord Pennington the hand of my younger sister."

"Many things are transferred at the tables, Mrs. Roberts." Fabric rustled as the woman shrugged. "The contracts are quite steadfast, for I retain the proper legal services regarding such things."

"Sybil is only nineteen!" Desperation rang in Adriana's voice. "She doesn't deserve to be wed to the likes of the earl."

"That is only your opinion. The final decision has already been made."

"But it's wrong!" In her verve to save her sister from the fate she despaired of, Adriana launched up from the sofa. She clutched her fists in the folds of her cloak. "Sybil is beautiful, Mrs. Dove-Lyon, a touch spoiled, but she has the chance to make a brilliant marriage. Please release her from the contracts that bind her to Lord Pennington. The worst man in London will never appreciate her for herself."

A low-pitched chuckle emanated from the proprietress. "Those are the terms to which your father and Lord Pennington agreed to before the last hand got underway that night."

Adriana heaved a sigh. "You won't release her." It wasn't a question.

"That depends. Do you have something of equal value to offer me in your sister's stead? After all, I must be able to profit from a new deal."

It was now or never. She forced a hard swallow into her suddenly dry throat. "*I* will marry Lord Pennington in Sybil's place."

"You?" Mrs. Dove-Lyon laughed outright at that. While it was a pleasant-enough sound, it sent gooseflesh sailing over her skin. "Whyever would I let you do that? Lord Pennington won't want *you*."

Indignation filled her chest in a hot wave. "Because I am old and have failed in every way a woman can?" The gall of this woman! "Or is it because I am possessed of more curves than men of the *ton* prefer?" These were all insecurities she couldn't quite conquer.

"There is nothing wrong with your looks or your age. In fact, many women don't come into their own until later in life. Furthermore, the idea that a woman must procreate to feel worthy is a ridiculous notion, so disabuse yourself of that. Come down from the boughs, Mrs. Roberts." Amusement wove through the command. "I meant that you are not Lord Pennington's usual type of woman."

That mollified her somewhat. "Honestly, Mrs. Dove-Lyon, I care not what the earl wants." The fact she'd never set eyes on the earl didn't matter. Who was he to judge a woman's worth on looks alone? With her strength suddenly sapped following her outburst, Adriana quickly reseated herself. "Please, put me in my sister's place. She has a future, where I do not. Her name remains untarnished, and her prospects will only grow bigger once I am away from the household."

"How does a change in arrangement benefit you beyond saving your sister?"

"It doesn't." She frowned and her chest hurt. Would her idea not work? "There is no respectable marriage for me. No hope of a family due to my age. I don't even expect to find love if this happens. In fact, I am not certain I believe in that emotion any longer." Her voice broke and she hated that weakness, but there was nothing for it. "I merely want an end to the struggle to make ends meet or the pitying and horror-filled glances."

The widow snorted. "Those looks will not cease if you take your sister's place. Lord Pennington is a man steeped in rumors and innuendo."

"It doesn't matter." Nothing did. "My future will be settled, as will Sybil's."

"And your father?"

She shrugged and hardened her heart against her parent. "Father can go hang. He made this mess, so he can find his own way out, but please, consider my offer."

"Your sacrifice, you mean?"

Why was it so dark in the room? Perhaps the widow preferred it that way, so no one could see her emotions or even her face and thus perpetuate her mystique. "Perhaps."

"Do you have any other requests?"

What else was there? Then she sighed. "If you grant me—or rather Sybil—this boon, please promise you will settle money on her allotted for two Seasons. That is all she will need to land a man high on the instep but make certain Father cannot have access to it."

"Of course." Fabric rustled. "You have a shrewd head for business, Mrs. Roberts." A hint of respect lingered in the other woman's voice.

"It has been accumulated out of experience and necessity."

"If I make this change, what do *I* receive in the deal? Because, as you must have surmised, the Lyon's Den always takes a cut of the winnings."

No wonder she was so successful, but Adriana racked her brain for something that would tip her hand. "You shall have the satisfaction of knowing that you have pulled the wool over the eyes of the worst man in London. I am quite certain he has won more from your establishment and seduced more women from your house here than you are comfortable with." She didn't know that for a fact, of course, but it was a fair guess.

"I am impressed, Mrs. Roberts." A genuine laugh escaped the woman shrouded in shadows. "Perhaps we will speak soon on other matters, but as for the one on the table at present…"

Adriana held her breath as she waited for the widow's next words.

"You and I have a deal. I will alter the betrothal contracts. You will take your sister's place and will marry Lord Pennington two days hence, and the special license will have your name upon it as well." She snapped her fingers.

Immediately, a door at the back of the room behind the widow opened.

Mrs. Dove-Lyon said, "Call for the solicitor. We need an amendment drawn up posthaste."

"At once," the whispered voice of a man said before he departed on silent feet.

Elation fought with worry in Adriana's chest. "Won't the earl be suspicious?"

"Of course not. My people have arranged everything, even in

procuring the license. And from what I understand, your sister's name was never given at the table."

Relief shuddered down her spine. "Thank you so much." She once more shot to her feet. "Is there anything else I should do?"

"Wear heavy veils at the ceremony, and your sister must *not* attend. That is key. If you can, stay away from your parents until after the ceremony. I'd rather not have your father get wind of the scheme until later."

"Not that he will care once he discovers you've funded Sybil's Seasons." Her muscles were no longer tense, but now that it was certain she would marry Lord Pennington in her sister's place, the urge to retch grew strong.

What have I done?

"You may go, Mrs. Roberts, and may this upcoming union be everything you wish it might be."

In a daze, Adriana stumbled out of the room, and was immediately intercepted by Helena, who led her through the house and then finally back to the street where a hired cab waited.

The last thing she wanted was another marriage to a horrible man, but better she than Sybil. Perhaps in this way, her family would finally be proud of her once everything was said and done.

CHAPTER THREE

October 14, 1817

MONTAGUE FAIRLY STEWED in hot annoyance and simmering anger. Not only had he won some unknown chit's hand in a card game, but he'd also been coerced into a quick marriage by Mrs. Dove-Lyon, through blackmail no less.

His jaw clenched and one hand curled into a fist with the memory of when he'd signed the betrothal contracts. The woman had had the gall to dangle his biggest secret in front of him, threatened to out him if he didn't comply, and that revelation would damage his reputation in ways his own self-destruction hadn't managed.

When he wasn't attending to the duties for his title, he took refuge as a painter of some minor acclaim… that grew with each piece he released. Under the *nom de plume* of Monsieur Depardieu, he created lifelike portraits of various ladies in the *ton*, a few heads of state and royalty, as well as the occasional oil landscape. For an extra fee, he did nudes of some of his mistresses, especially the ones with a title and compelling enough charms. Every painting he did while donning the persona and disguise of a Frenchman, and he continued to do so for his own entertainment.

Other men bought the paintings—including the risqué ones—and sometimes the subjects bought them. Montague had made a tidy income to pass the time, and the coin therein usually accompanied him to the gaming tables, for in that way, he never touched what was in his coffers. Painting helped to pass the time and quiet his mind. Additionally, he adored the challenge of it and the concentration on the tasks helped him to forget his abject grief or anger.

Yet Mrs. Dove-Lyon had exploited that, ferreted out the secret—God only knew how—and had used it against him so he would marry this young lady without a chance to escape.

And in the process, she'd made that outlet for peace feel like something to be ashamed of. For that, he could never forgive her.

Now, as he stood in his drawing room, contemplating having a fourth drink of the morning—and it not yet ten-thirty—his best friend strolled over to him while guests gathered within the room.

"You look like a dog's breakfast," Ashbury said without ceremony. Of course, he was dressed in the first stare of fashion with his blond locks arranged in a popular style. No existing on a few hours' sleep for him.

"And a good morning to you," he grumbled in response. He'd had four days to acclimate to this event, but that hadn't happened. In mere moments, his life would change against his will, all because he'd lost a hand of faro that he could swear had been dictated by the proprietress of the Lyon's Den in that house's favor.

I do not lose.

Yet, he had no evidence to prove the cheating or rather manipulation, and now he would be married because of it.

Damn and blast.

The viscount lifted an eyebrow. "You haven't come 'round to accepting this union." It wasn't a question.

"Why should I? I don't want this; I've *never* wanted this."

"You did at one time. Twice, actually," Ashbury was quick to remind him.

"That was then." A muscle in his jaw ticced. "I was in love with each of my fiancées. There is nothing like that here. And it's being forced besides."

Such manipulation didn't sit well with him. Yes, his power as an earl meant he could make life difficult for Mrs. Dove-Lyon. However, she wielded power of her own, and had for some time, and the last thing he needed was her mucking about further into his affairs. The fact she'd already discovered one of his secrets rankled, for he didn't let very many people close. Hell, even Ashbury didn't know about the paintings.

"In all honesty, I'm glad you are in the thick of this Drury Lane drama and not me." He crossed his arms at his chest while watching a few more guests filter into the room. "Being leg-shackled is daunting enough; but being forced to wed a bride you don't know? It's untenable."

Montague frowned. "Interesting choice of words."

"Why?"

"You said 'being leg-shackled is daunting enough' instead of 'sounds like' it might be." He stared harder at his best friend. "Have you been married before?"

A faint flush rose up over Ashbury's collar. "That is a story for another day, and not suitable for the morning of your wedding."

What the devil did that mean? The man hadn't confirmed or denied the inquiry. "Regardless, when it's your time, I hope your mess is just as large as this one, but whatever you do, stay well away from Mrs. Dove-Lyon. I believe that woman delights in ordering us all about as if we were marionettes on strings."

"Yes, well, I've always warned you about spending so much time at the Lyon's Den. I don't believe it's merely a gaming hell." Ashbury gestured to someone across the room with his chin. "Not that Mrs. Dove-Lyon is a witch, but she's not just the owner of that establishment."

Montague snorted as he followed his friend's line of vision. The proprietress had entered the room. She took a chair in a grouping toward the back of the room, and though she wore a semi-opaque veil, there was no question of her identity. "Ah, come to make certain I go through it, eh?" he asked softly. "I despise this so much." His life was no longer his own. Again, anger welled in his chest like a hot wave that would soon destroy him if he wasn't careful.

"Perhaps this union won't be as horrid as you fear." Ashbury looked about. "Where is Satan today?"

"The cat, much like his owner, despises people in his home, so he is cowering beneath a bed somewhere." How would the feline like the intrusion of having a mistress suddenly about? That remained to be seen.

"Poor kitty. You and he will have quite the time of it." The viscount clapped a hand to his shoulder. "Will you stay in Town after the ceremony?"

"No. I had planned to remove to my estate in Essex." It had been an age since he'd been to the area, and he rather missed the sea. The rhythmic sounds of the waves gave a certain amount of peace to his seething soul.

Ashbury frowned. "Why?"

He shrugged. "Why not?"

"You should stay in Town. There is more to do here, and I can keep an eye on you."

"For your own amusement, I would imagine."

"Of course." The viscount shot him a cheeky grin. "This is certain to be the scandal of the decade, knowing you." He waggled his eyebrows. "Perhaps this marriage is what you need to free you from the miasma of guilt and grief you are currently lost in."

How the devil would marrying a woman he didn't know help? Especially when he was denied unions with either of his fiancées—the women he'd actually loved. "What if I don't want out? I don't want to forget."

"Ah." The other man looked on with a mixture of pity and empathy in his eyes, which irritated Montague more. "Keep an open mind. I miss my friend, Pennington, as well as the days when we regularly saw each other or prowled ballrooms." He offered a faint grin. "Don't let grief and depression pull you under." Again, he touched Montague's shoulder. "Promise me you will try to make the union work… swim to the surface, as it were."

He sighed. Truly, he missed the man he used to be years ago as well, yet how could he return to that man without having his heart broken, his soul destroyed? Having a spouse forced upon him would prove a huge inconvenience and put both him and her at risk. Above everything, he would guard his heart; she wouldn't have any part of it.

Time and history had taught him that love or soft feelings were disastrous.

Finally, he said, "I will try, but I can make no guarantees."

"Good." Then Ashbury cleared his throat. "There is your bride. It would seem we've run out of time."

Bloody hell.

As murmurs went through the room, Montague's pulse accelerated, not with anticipation but with aggravation. He turned to glance at the woman who'd entered—the woman he would soon bind himself to in the eyes of the law.

It was impossible to tell what she looked like, for she wore a navy, long-sleeved gown with tulle at the bodice. Silver embroidery work decorated the hem and waist. Heavy navy veils obscured her face and back as if she were a grieving widow, but she was quite short, perhaps only a couple of inches over five feet. The baron and his wife trailed behind her. Wasn't there another daughter? Apparently, she had decided not to come.

He peered at Ashbury. "What the deuce?" he whispered.

"I have no idea. Perhaps she's shy?"

"Or hideous." Perhaps the baron had lied about the chit's looks. Had she done this to make a point? That wedding him would mean her demise?

"There is that, but you are out of time, my friend. Good luck." Then the viscount left him as the baron led his daughter over to Montague.

"Pennington."

"Kentwood." He frowned at the man who had no idea how to play cards to the detriment of his daughter's future. For the moment, he ignored the girl in the veils. "I'm surprised you haven't tried to manipulate more coin from me."

Confusion shadowed the older man's face. "I'm sure I don't know to what you are referring."

Of course he didn't. Montague had lost heavily during that last hand which had landed him here, and when he'd signed the contracts under Mrs. Dove-Lyon's eagle eyes, he'd been encouraged to set aside funding for two Seasons. Apparently, the other daughter deserved a chance to find wedded bliss, and without coin from her father, that was next to impossible. A dowry gift of sorts.

He was saved from a response when a man of indeterminate years dressed in black approached. He was no doubt the vicar.

"Can I assume you are Lord Pennington?" the man inquired in a voice as smooth as glass.

"I am."

"Ah, good. I'm pleased to meet you. I am Mr. Padgett, the vicar who will oversee your nuptial ceremony." The clergyman gestured with his chin to a young man who'd gone to sit by Mrs. Dove-Lyon. "That is my clerk, Mr. Dodson. The register will be handled by him." He transferred a much-used copy of the *Book of Common Prayer* as he glanced at Miss Stapleton. "Good morning."

"Hullo." There weren't enough words there to know what her

voice truly sounded like. She neither looked at the vicar or at him. Was she grateful for the union or was she just as outraged she'd been forced into it as he?

The baron cleared his throat. "Well, I shall just sit next to my wife." Awkwardly, he touched his daughter's shoulder. "Uh, I hope you are happy in your new life."

Miss Stapleton didn't answer.

How exceedingly odd, but it answered his question. She was furious. Her taut posture and the way her fingers curled into fists indicated that.

The vicar frowned. "Shall we begin?"

Montague snorted. "Best have this over with before the family attempts to swindle even more coin from me."

From beside him, a gasp issued beneath the veils. Had he offended her? Well, good. She had to know that none of this was fair.

With a speculative glance at them both, Mr. Padgett led them to the top of the room, pausing before the fireplace where cheerful flames danced behind the decorative metal grate, for there was an autumnal chill in the air. "If everyone could please take a seat? The nuptial couple is ready to begin." He included them both in his gaze. "Lord Pennington, Miss Stapleton, please face me." When they did, he opened his book to the appropriate page. "Dearly beloved, we are gathered together here in the sight of God, and in the face of these witnesses, to join together this Man and this Woman in holy Matrimony; which is an honorable estate, instituted of God in the time of man's innocency, signifying unto us the mystical union that is betwixt Christ and his Church…"

Montague forced a hard swallow into his throat and attempted to concentrate on the pulse pounding in his ears. Perhaps it would drown out the vicar's words. This wasn't how he'd wished to find himself wed. *Dear God*, in minutes he would say vows to this woman—this stranger—whose hand he'd won at a card table. He would be expected to begin a life with her, perhaps get her with child so that he could have his heir. Pain welled in his chest and sent sharp pricks of aching fire through his heart. If fate had been kind, he would have already been married seven years ago to the woman whom he'd actually loved. Oh, that would have been a grand life indeed, but now, he was being forced into this, a life with a woman he knew not at all. Hell, he didn't even have a clue as to what her Christian name was.

It was never supposed to end like any of this!

He wasn't supposed to be left alone, a hurting recluse who'd turned to many vices in order to keep reality at bay, yet here he was. At the last second, he stifled a wild sob that rose in his throat.

The woman at his side must have heard or suspected part of his distress, for she turned her head. With the heavy veils, he couldn't see her face let alone meet her gaze, but he wondered what she was thinking all the same.

The vicar continued, his voice a pleasing timbre as he talked about the holy state they were about to embark upon. Montague wished he had a drink in hand, but that hardly seemed proper during what should be such an important event.

I don't want to do this! It felt all too wrong, a betrayal to the memories of his dead fiancées.

Mr. Padgett held his prayer book in his hands, the black leather spine cracked and worn, while he addressed Montague. "Wilt thou have this Woman to thy wedded Wife, to live together after God's ordinance in the holy estate of Matrimony?" His lips curved with a smile. The poor sot assumed this was a wanted union. "Wilt thou love her, comfort her, honor her, and keep her in sickness and in health; and, forsaking all others, keep thee only unto her, so long as ye both shall live?"

Oh, God.

A knot of unshed emotion formed in his throat. *I most certainly will never love this woman.* Never again would he allow himself to become that vulnerable, that hopeful. "I…" How could he say those words when he didn't mean them? With a quick glance over his shoulder, his gaze landed on Mrs. Dove-Lyon. Was it his imagination or did one of her eyebrows quirk upward? Impossible to tell beneath the black veil. Then he cleared his throat. "I will," he uttered from around clenched teeth.

"Very good," Mr. Padgett said. He put a forefinger to the words on one page as he addressed Miss Stapleton. "Wilt thou have this Man to thy wedded Husband, to live together after God's ordinance in the holy estate of Matrimony? Wilt thou obey him, and serve him, love him, honor him, and keep him in sickness and in health; and, forsaking all others, keep thee only unto him, so long as ye both shall live?"

For the space of more than a few heartbeats, the woman at his side remained silent. Her left hand curled into a fist, but she hid it into her skirting. In little more than a raspy whisper, she said, "I will, though it's anyone's guess if I shall *obey* the worst man in London's dictates."

"What?" Her additional words took Montague by surprise. Again, he peered at her, but the heavy veils prevented him from seeing her face. Yes, there was no question the woman loathed him, and he had nothing to do with this!

"You heard me," she said in response with the same hushed voice that was rather husky and had odd shivers moving down his spine.

"Everyone has their flaws, and reputations notwithstanding, this *is* a holy occasion," Mr. Padgett said as confusion shadowed his face. He then instructed Montague to take her right hand in his right, which he then did, and Miss Stapleton's hand shook. Was she nervous or enraged? "Lord Pennington, please repeat after me…"

With solicitous attention, he made an effort to memorize the handful of words through the growing haze of annoyance and anger building through his person. "I, Montague Andrew Bassage, Earl of Pennington, take thee Miss Adriana Louise Stapleton as my wedded Wife, to have and to hold from this day forward, for better for worse, for richer for poorer, in sickness and in health, to love and to cherish, until death us do part…" His throat tightened as he spoke those most sacred of words that would forever bind him with her, the eventuality that had the power to completely break him for a third time if he didn't keep his wits about him, but at least he knew her name now, "… according to God's holy ordinance; and thereto I plight thee my troth."

"It is good to see emotion when a man recites vows." Obviously, Mr. Padgett assumed he was overcome with affection for his bride-to-be.

From somewhere behind him, Kentwood began a protest, but then someone quelled his words. Montague couldn't summon enough interest to glance his way.

"Please release hands. Lord Pennington, take her left in your left hand." Once they'd done as instructed, he trained his attention on the woman at his side. "Miss Stapleton, repeat after me." He gave her the words, much like the ones he'd said to Montague moments before.

The veils obscured everything above her bosom, which was quite full, and perhaps in a different lifetime, he might have lusted after those charms. "I, Miss Adriana Stapleton take thee Montague Andrew Bassage, Lord Pennington, as my wedded Husband." Her voice broke on the last word. Was she overcome due to having landed a titled gentleman or in anguish that she hated every moment of this ceremony? Damn those heavy veils!

Again, the baron uttered a word of protest, but was quickly subdued. Perhaps he regretted what he had done at the gaming table. Fabric rustled, footsteps echoed. No doubt someone had ushered him from the room.

The woman at Montague's side continued. "To have and to hold from this day forward, for better for worse, for richer for poorer, in sickness and in health, to love, cherish, and to obey, 'until death us do part, according to God's holy ordinance." A suspicious sound that was much like a sob emanated from her. "And thereto I give thee my troth."

"It seems our nuptial couple is quite emotional this morning." Mr. Padgett grinned. Ignorance was apparently bliss. Lines framed his eyes and mouth. "Please release your hands." To Montague, he whispered, "Now is the time to offer up a ring and any respects you might have for my services."

"Of course, for why wouldn't the church also separate me from my coin?" Bitterness fairly dripped from his voice. He dug a ring from the pocket of his waistcoat, which he gave to the vicar, who rested it upon his open *Book of Common Prayer* while Montague followed it with a small leather pouch as payment and gratuity for services rendered. In the light of the October morning, the square-cut emerald winked. Two small round diamonds—one on either side—twinkled. The piece had long been part of the Pennington jewels, and eventually this woman would have the rest of the parure, but a muscle in his cheek ticced to know he was giving it to someone he knew not at all.

"Thank you, Your Lordship." Mr. Padgett murmured a few words, no doubt as a blessing, before returning the bauble to him as his bride removed the glove from her left hand. "You may present the ring to the lady." As soon as Montague slipped it onto the fourth finger of Miss Stapleton's hand, the vicar spoke again, the words directed to him. "Please repeat after me."

A shudder went down Montague's spine. He hadn't the luck to wed his previous fiancées, and yet here he was, doing exactly that with *her*. There was no going back now. Miss Stapleton's hand shook in his. "With this Ring I thee wed, with my Body I thee worship, and with all my worldly Goods I thee endow. In the Name of the Father, and of the Son, and of the Holy Ghost. Amen."

Dear God, he would be expected to lie with this woman, when all he wished to do was hide himself away to mourn the life he was leaving behind, mourn for the life he'd wanted once upon a time.

In the silence following, Miss Stapleton huffed, which ruffled the veils. "You will absolutely have *no* access to my body, Your Lordship," she warned in such a low voice that he was obliged to lean closer in order to hear. "I didn't want this union but had no choice." In a few tugs, she had the glove back on her hand.

Yes, well, at least we have that in common. Still, her statement rankled. Did she not understand what was expected of them? Of *her* now that she was his countess?

Mr. Padgett cleared his throat. "Please kneel while everyone is invited to pray with me."

Montague did so but didn't much care if she came down with him. Anger raged within his chest, and he let it, for this was just another obstacle strewn in his path. As the words of the prayer flowed over him, he dared to peek at his new bride. Her head was cast downward, but emotion fairly seethed from her in waves. Then the prayer was over, and Montague stood. So did Miss Stapleton, er rather the new Lady Pennington.

Mr. Padgett closed his book. "I now pronounce thee husband and wife."

Spattered applause broke out among the gathered guests. No doubt most in attendance remained puzzled over the hasty nuptials.

"If you'll please see my clerk to sign the register, then everything will be official," Mr. Padgett said with a slight grin.

Before Montague could say anything, his wife turned toward him. With shaking hands, she lifted her veils and put them back behind her head. For the first time, he was able to see her face. Loathing glinted in doe-brown eyes. Annoyance lined her round face that was as voluptuous as the rest of her frame. Blonde hair had been pinned up in pleasing twists and curls, her full lips were set in a thin line, but the thing that shocked him to his soul was the fact this woman was definitely *not* a nineteen-year-old chit.

Wasn't she supposed to be thin and brunette? At least that was the rumor, and her father had hinted as much. Then the horror of what had happened dawned on him. Anger surged, hot and fierce, in his chest. *Bloody hell.* "What sort of deviltry is this?" Now he knew why the other sister hadn't attended the ceremony. "You are not the woman I was to wed."

She snorted in derision. "Yes, well, you are not the man I would have chosen either, but we don't always have what we want in this life, Lord Pennington." Her gaze snapped brown lightning. "At least I saved my sister from a life as your wife."

"Damn it all to hell." Rage swept unchecked through his veins as he turned his back on his new bride. He assessed the room at large, and as many of the attendees stared wide-eyed at him—the baron and his wife were suspiciously absent—he stalked over the floor until he reached Mrs. Dove-Lyon's location before she could escape through the open drawing room doors. "*You* did this!" He didn't care that his raised voice echoed through the space and made him seem like the beast gossips often likened him to.

A chuckle came from the widow. "Of course I did. You were there; you signed the contracts, and if I remember correctly, you voiced no objections at that time."

This is untenable! He shoved a gloved hand through his hair. "You deliberately tricked me."

"I merely took the better offer from Miss Stapleton, or rather Mrs. Roberts as she was known before you married her." The owner of the Lyon's Den coughed softly while some of the guests continued to gawk.

That name was vaguely familiar. He racked his mind for the reason why, but only came up with gossip. "You have made a misstep, madam," he said in a voice graveled with rage. "I will see you brought low for this, send fire and brimstone against the Lyon's Den."

"I rather think you won't." Below the veil's hem, her lips curved into a wicked smile. "I'm fairly certain I can do more damage to *you*."

With a laugh, she moved around him. "Enjoy your wedding night, Lord Pennington. I have no doubts it will prove… enlightening."

What the devil did that mean?

Not knowing, and certainly not in a mood to talk with anyone in the room, Montague shot a look at Ashbury and then exited through a different door. There was no way out. He'd been trapped, quite neatly, and it was worse than he'd assumed. He'd married a woman steeped in scandal, an alleged murderess, and not in his usual style.

He didn't stop his flight until he reached his library, where he shut himself away. In order to contain his temper and tamp down his rage, he needed a drink—or three. The damned wedding breakfast could wait.

What the hell am I supposed to do now?

CHAPTER FOUR

ADRIANA PACED THE floor of the suite of rooms set aside at Bassage House for its countess, situated across the corridor from the earl's rooms. A smaller bedroom occupied each side of the hall as well. Presumably for guests, though she doubted if Pennington ever entertained. She hadn't seen her new husband since the wedding breakfast that morning—twelve hours ago—when he'd made a brief appearance, and was as apparently as livid as she'd been. It had been her first glimpse of the man and the beast the rumors likened him to; they weren't far off. He had quite the snarling, snapping temper.

With a huff of annoyance, she glanced about the well-appointed bedchamber done in pleasing colors of rose and gold with all the luxuries a woman holding the title of countess could ever desire. Her parents had delivered her meager possessions to the house when they'd arrived for the nuptial ceremony—no need to pay someone to transfer the two trunks over. *Good Lord, I'm a countess now. What will that entail?* She truly had no idea, for she'd been cheated out of a long engagement or even a courtship, and she'd certainly not mingled within the *beau monde* enough to glean that knowledge.

She paused at the window and peered outside. It was too dark to see much of the square or the greenspace connected to the St. James address, and she rather preferred that view over Pennington's, which undoubtedly overlooked the Mayfair streets. At least this would provide an oasis of sorts. The muscles in her belly tightened with anxiety. How would she survive this new life wed to the worst man in London?

Married. Again. And not even to a better man than she'd had before.

Her new husband might hold a title and wield a fair amount of power within the *ton*, but she'd seen how he'd exhibited himself after the nuptial ceremony when he'd confronted Mrs. Dove-Lyon the second Adriana had revealed her identity. In a way, it had been satisfying that he hadn't managed to bully or rout her in any way. Adriana twisted the emerald ring that sat upon the fourth finger of her left hand. However, in another, it only drove home the perils she now faced being the wife of a man possessed of such depth of emotion.

A man she knew next to nothing about outside of rumors.

What am I going to do?

The only saving grace was that she'd removed Sybil from having this same fate. Had her sister thanked her as she'd departed the townhouse for the nuptial ceremony earlier? Of course not. She'd only pouted because she'd not been allowed to come, for obvious reasons. And neither had her parents expressed gratitude when they'd departed after the breakfast had concluded. They'd wished her luck and left with expressions of relief. Though her mother might have said something, her father had more or less hustled her from the house.

Another huff escaped Adriana and she once more turned her attention to the window. Across the way, the gas lamps on the street at the opposite side of the square drew her notice. Were the people who occupied this area of Mayfair happy in their lives? Or had they, like her, been forced into an existence they didn't want and had no control over?

She didn't know; would probably never know, but she continued to gaze out that window regardless.

A scratching on the door to the adjoining dressing room broke her from the thoughts. "Will you wish for assistance in undressing, Your Ladyship?"

The title, still foreign to her, made Adriana frown all the more. She turned to peer at the young lady's maid she'd been assigned, a girl probably not older than Sybil, who had dark hair and pretty blue eyes. "No thank you, Bess. I don't have anything fancy or even appropriate for a wedding night in any case." It was why she hadn't changed out of the navy gown. There were no pretty embroidered underthings or even delicate, frothy night gowns, for the Stapleton coffers were to let and there hadn't been time, besides, to gather such things even if they'd had the coin. Lord knew her reprobate first husband hadn't left her with the means to look after herself.

Curiosity lined the younger woman's face. "Is there anything I can bring you? A tray of food, tea? I noticed you haven't eaten since this morning." There was no judgment in her expression, merely befuddlement, as if she couldn't quite understand what type of person her new mistress was.

Had she heard the horrible rumors surrounding her name too?

Tamping down the urge to sigh, Adriana offered a small, tight smile. "I am well enough right now. Thank you." She didn't feel like eating. In fact, the thought of food made her stomach roil. Her nerves were much too taut for that. "I imagine after I speak with the earl, I'll retire for the night."

Surely her prospects would seem better in the morning.

The maid nodded. "If you need me, just ring. And…"

"Yes?"

"Well, my lady, I meant it might take a bit to rub along well with His Lordship." A blush stained her cheeks. "He is a difficult man to be around, but perhaps he has his reasons."

Now that *was* interesting. "How long have you been a part of his staff?"

She shrugged. "A few years, but I'm glad now to have been promoted to a lady's maid." When she smiled, her eyes twinkled. "I hope I make you proud."

Adriana's heart went out to her. Wasn't that what everyone wanted from various people in their lives? "I am certain we'll get on well together. Goodnight, Bess." Perhaps later, as time went on, she could befriend a few of the servants and discover all the horrible secrets the earl was keeping and why.

"Goodnight, Your Ladyship." With a tiny wave, the girl exited the room.

Once more, she was alone with her thoughts.

What kind of man was the Earl of Pennington? Could she believe the gossip and rumors, or like the ones surrounding her, were they not quite the full truth? She hadn't had the time to discuss what sort of union they would share or the expectations therein, but as of this moment, she vastly preferred a marriage of convenience, for she had had her fill of vile men, drunk men, or really men in general.

And if he couldn't square with that, then they would start their life together with horns locked. It didn't matter much to her. Before she could decide what to do, a dart of movement out of the corner of her eye caught her attention. It could very well have been a shadow, but when she trained her gaze on it, the dark spot slowly became the form of a cat.

"Hello there," she crooned to the feline. When it brushed against the leg of the bedside table, she crouched and held out a hand. "Come here, pretty baby."

The entirely black cat looked at her with the most gorgeous green eyes and uttered a soft mewl. In welcome or warning?

"What are you doing here? Surely you don't belong to that horrible earl." As the feline slowly came close, Adriana drew her fingers along its sleek head then she scratched behind one of the soft ears. "What is your name, I wonder."

The door to the corridor swung open and Lord Pennington stood—or rather swayed—in the frame. "Leave Satan alone." The thunderous order echoed off the walls.

With a bushy tail from fright, the cat darted from the room.

Interesting name, that, but no doubt the earl found it a joke.

"Oh, goodness." The whisper sounded overly loud in the sudden silence, as if his presence had sucked all the energy from the room. He was certainly more darkly handsome than he'd been at the ceremony, and quite rugged looking now that he'd shed his jacket and waistcoat.

Indeed, there was a fascination, an undeniable charisma about him in this stage of undress. His hair lay in a riot of curls about his head as if he'd shoved his fingers through those brown tresses in frustration more than a few times. In the illumination from the lamp, touches of gray glimmered within them. The evening stubble that shadowed his cheeks and sharp jaw had unexpected tremors of interest sailing down her spine. And those eyes! Good heavens, the blue-gray depths were as angry as a storm at sea as he raked that gaze up and down her person. Long fingers clutched a brandy bottle that was half-emptied.

Yes, he was handsome as sin just now, but he was also firmly in his cups.

And in a wicked fury.

Cold disappointment twisted down her spine. So much for the small hope that he might prove different than his previous behavior.

"Let's have this over with, then." As soon as he moved further into the room, he slammed the door closed behind him. That damning echo would forever ring in her ears. Then he set the bottle on a nearby rose-inlaid table. "Need an heir in any event." Even his frown heightened his attractiveness. "Didn't want any of this, though." Drunk enough to have hit the rambling stage but not quite inebriated enough to slur his words.

Delightful. The word bounced through her mind, borne on a heavy push of sarcasm.

And apparently, he was well on his way to being out of his mind. Adriana scuttled away as he advanced. "I barely know you, but I suspect even if I did, I would never have you into my bed." She glared when the words had no effect. "I thought I'd made myself abundantly clear earlier today."

The earl grunted. "Should have thought about that before you deceived me at the altar." He set about removing his cuffs, collar, and cravat. The items fell indiscriminately to the plush Aubusson carpet like dollops of cream. "You and that Mrs. Dove-Lyon. Wretched woman. Took my blunt and then gave me... *this.*" He gestured to her with a hand as if she was naught but an outcast in the street.

How rude!

"Well, I couldn't have you defile my innocent sister."

He leered. "Not in the habit of taking virgins into my bed."

"Half of London knows exactly what sort of woman you *prefer* in your bed, Pennington," she said and couldn't quite leave the sarcasm to her thoughts. Out of all the men she could have taken for a second husband, she had chosen to have *this man*, who had apparently not cared that he'd made womanizing a challenge for all other rakes. When she crossed her arms beneath her breasts, his gaze dropped to her décolletage. Of course it did. "Sybil has the chance to make someone proud more than I do. She's not the one steeped in scandal, and I couldn't in good conscience send her into the lion's mouth as it were."

It took immense willpower not to snort in ironic laughter, for that damned Lyon's Den gambling hall had convoluted everything.

Pennington frowned. "Siblings are often not the same." Again, he raked his gaze up and down her person with an intensity that sent shivers sailing over her skin. "Since I have not seen her, I'll assume your sister is the beautiful one." He shrugged. "You are not. Life goes on."

"Argh!" The man was naught but a bounder. As much as she wished to slap that lazy grin from his face, she held back. This time. "You needn't be crass. If that advice is even penetrating the haze of brandy you've dunked yourself into."

Good grief but she despised men who drank their troubles away. It spoke of weak character.

Annoyance flashed across his face. Those dark eyes of his glittered. "What I do with my time is not your concern." The earl closed the distance between them, caught her chin in an unmovable grip, and then bent his head and gave her an open-mouthed kiss that was more slobber than skill.

This is outside of enough! Adriana wrenched away, and with her other hand, wiped at the moisture on her chin. Rage danced down her spine. How dare he! The first kiss from her new husband was an absolute travesty and decidedly unwanted. A trace of fear circled through her belly, for she'd been taken against her will a handful of times by her first husband. *I won't stand for it again.* She shoved at his chest until he disengaged from her. "You reek of spirits and your brain is pickled."

"And you are an old, dried-up prude who probably despises a man's touch," he spat out and sent a glance to the brandy bottle on the table.

Bastard. "When a sober man touches me, I shall have something to compare my experience to. Now, if you'll show yourself out?" As she shook from both anger and fear, she went to step around him, but he clamped a hand about her wrist with a grip like iron. Her mouth went dry. Surely, he wasn't an abusive man, not if he had as many mistresses as rumored. Someone would have complained about such treatment. "Let me go, Lord Pennington." Ice had formed in her voice.

No longer was she a naïve woman who thought it had been her lot in life to make excuses for and suffer at the hands of a drunk.

"Since you orchestrated this marriage, I expect you to see the charade through to the bitter end." His tone brooked no argument, and his hold never wavered.

"And I expect you to act like a gentleman." Her words were just as frosty. For long moments, she stared him down, daring him almost, for she *would* slap him. Despite the fact he was three sheets to the wind, there was something compelling about this man that tugged at her curiosity and even her empathy, which worked to further irritate her. And drat if he didn't smell divine, all cedar and citrus and spice over and above the brandy.

"I haven't been a gentleman for a long time," he responded, and the low pitch of his voice sent an unexpected thrill of awareness over her skin. His gaze dropped to her breasts. "Take off your clothes, Countess."

"Oh, *such* a romantic you are, Pennington." She pointed her gaze to the ceiling as she shook her head. "At least give it some stick."

"No such thing as romance. Not anymore." But he released her wrist.

She forced a hard swallow into her suddenly dry throat. "Why do you think that?" It was a good opportunity for her to perhaps learn about him.

"It doesn't matter." His expression was inscrutable.

"I'll wager it does, deep down." She watched him, still wary. Men in their cups were unpredictable at best. "I had hoped I could have that in my first marriage. I thought I could have come to love my husband despite the fact he wasn't a good man." Emotion thickened her voice. "But it was nothing more than a foolish dream, and even as old or as prudish or dried out that you assume I am, I persist in dreaming once in a while." A tiny, self-deprecating laugh escaped her. "A character flaw, if you will."

Oh, why had she told him that? He didn't care, and that would only make her vulnerable.

Something flickered in his eyes, but she couldn't read it. He was all too skilled in hiding his true self. "Dreams are as foolish as romance. That I know for certain." When the earl raised his gaze to her face, a blank mask was once more in place. What didn't he want her to know? "You wanted this union; it matters not why. Now you'll pay for it by giving me an heir." Once more, he attempted to kiss her, but stumbled. His lips glanced along her cheek.

"I hardly think you'll make a good father if you persist in conducting your affairs as you have been." Adriana put distance between them. "Bearing a child is quite personal and is a choice. Not something to be forced onto a woman." The ache in her chest returned. "But if you must know, conceiving a child is beyond my ken." With each word, she hated herself for that failure. "If you want an heir, I'll prove a disappointment."

"What?" That stopped him for a second. He gawked at her. "You are barren?"

Quick tears sprang to her eyes. "So it would seem."

"Another deception." A hint of desolation shadowed his face but vanished under new determination. "No matter. This union will be consummated, for there is truly no escape."

"Why are you so annoying?" Obviously, she wouldn't have compassion or support from this man. Adriana crawled onto the bed, for it was the quickest way to have something as a shield. "Let me make this abundantly clear to you, Lord Pennington. I didn't want this union any more than you did. Now we are both trapped."

"Agreed. All of this can be laid at your feet."

She snorted. "Who was the one at that gaming table?"

"Again, not my fault your father cannot play cards."

"That's beside the point." If he refused to acknowledge his part in this debacle, they were at an impasse. "Best keep this to a marriage of convenience and we can go our separate ways soon enough. You can shuttle me off to an estate, tucked away so no one can see, and I won't mind in the least because I won't be with you. A boorish earl who acts like a veritable beast. No sane bride wants that."

"Damn fool woman. What do you know of it?" To her horror, the earl joined her on the bed, moved toward the edge that would block her escape. Her heartbeat raced. This scenario was all too reminiscent of the last time she'd seen her first husband alive. While she crawled over the pillows, he watched her with hooded eyes. "You are afraid of me." It wasn't a question.

"What do you think?" Her breath came in soft pants. "I survived one abusive man. I don't want another." It had been three years since she'd been free of that nightmare. Had she landed in an even bigger one?

That remained to be seen.

In the dim light, sorrow pooled in those dark depths, but why? "Bah." He shoved a hand through his hair and then stared at his fingers as if they were fascinating. "You are too fleshy in any event. The women I take to my bed do *not* look like you, don't act like you, *aren't*... you."

Before she could respond, Pennington slumped face down on the bed, apparently finally rendered unconscious by the brandy.

"Well, then." Adriana bit her bottom lip in an effort to stave off the tears that were imminent. She might not want him or this marriage, but she still had silly dreams of romance that her first marriage hadn't been able to kill. "I had hoped you wouldn't have acted like you did, so I guess we are both destined for disappointment," she whispered with tears prickling the backs of her eyelids.

Slowly, carefully, she slipped from the bed but kept her gaze on him. In slumber, her husband looked so... vulnerable and a bit lost. What had happened in his life to make him so? She didn't know but aimed to discover his secrets whether he wished her to or not.

As he snored on—the sound was quite annoying—she undressed for the night. Once she'd finished ablutions for the evening and had braided the long length of her blonde hair, Adriana crawled beneath the bedclothes. She turned down the lamp on the bedside table, dropped a pillow onto the floor, and then gave the earl a few targeted shoves until he tumbled onto the hardwood in a large thud with his head perfectly on the pillow.

"May you find the peace in slumber that eludes you while awake, Pennington." Then she turned over onto her side and squirmed to the opposite side of the bed from where he was located. His snores echoed eerily beneath that piece of furniture. Oddly, they were slightly comforting as she closed her eyes. Despite her best efforts to contain them or hold them back, silent tears leaked down her cheeks, for once again, she mourned for the life she'd never been given an opportunity to live.

Tomorrow was a new day where she would try to puzzle out the rest of her existence in this new and somewhat frightening role.

CHAPTER FIVE

October 15, 1817

ONTAGUE CAME AWAKE for the mere fact that his body was cold. Why? His bed was usually cozy with goose down during the chilly months. As he became more aware of his surroundings, he frowned. His head ached from a hangover.

Why the devil was he on the floor, and for that matter, why wasn't he in his own bedchamber?

In the gloom of the pre-dawn, he groaned as fragments of memories came back to him. The nuptial ceremony of yesterday morning. Embittered drinking with Ashbury following the wedding breakfast at his club. Returning home and then seeking out his new bride while he'd been deep in his cups.

And she'd immediately put a stop to any sort of advances he'd made while under the influence. Damn if he could remember what he'd done. There was a vague sense of trying to kiss her, but other than that, his mind remained trapped in a haze.

The effort of remembering enhanced the ache in his head, and when a slight rustle of the bedclothes echoed through the quiet, he rose up onto his knees in an effort to peek over the side of the bed. For a few seconds, he couldn't place the woman tucked beneath the covers with her blonde braid, strawberries-and-cream complexion, and a mouth relaxed in sleep; the lower lip slightly fuller than the top.

The memory of heavy navy veils danced through his mind and a shocking revelation. A slow grin spread over his face. Ah, this was his wife, and she'd apparently kicked him—quite literally—out of her bed the night before.

Slowly, so he wouldn't startle her awake, Montague slipped into the bed beside her. Then he realized that Satan had somehow snuck into the room, for he was curled into a tight, black ball of fluff on a pillow on her other side.

"Traitor," he whispered to the cat, who studiously ignored him.

Yes, he remained angry about being forced into a union, but he would be remiss if he didn't at least examine the face and form of the woman he'd taken to wife. To say nothing of being randy as hell. Though he'd apparently had the maggot in his brain last night to get her with child, that sentiment no longer held true this morning, especially after her startling revelation. It didn't negate the fact he would eventually need an heir, but he refused to revisit that possibility in the moment. Surely the Bassage line wouldn't die with him?

As he carefully moved the sheet and counterpane away from her body, the faint scent of lilacs rose to greet him. Not the sophisticated perfumes that some of the women he'd known previously wore, but it was intoxicating in its simplicity, nonetheless. And also unlike the other women he'd known, she was anything but tall, willowy, or brunette. In her state of relaxation, her generous curves were visible through the thin and quite plain fabric of her shift.

Awareness of her as a woman tingled over him to bring his shaft to life. Over the past handful of years, he'd made himself into the image of a careless rake, and he wouldn't be true to that image if he didn't have some sort of reaction to this woman—his wife—but he reminded himself that as soon as they could hold a decent conversation, he would send her on to his estate in Essex. Perhaps she would enjoy the seaside.

It didn't matter to him, but he couldn't have her underfoot. He didn't need a wife or a partner at his side, for there was nothing he could give to her.

There *was* nothing of him, for his heart and soul died long ago, but she was his wife, and they would need to make the best of it when they were together.

Except they couldn't do that if he sent her away.

His thoughts were too convoluted to sort just now.

Despite the pounding in his head, despite the annoyance that still raged hot in his chest, Montague joined her on the bed, leaned over her—damn, what was her name?—for that nugget of information had escaped him, and pressed his lips to hers.

In her sleep, she made a soft sound of welcome or encouragement, it was too difficult to say, but he took it in the spirit in which it was offered. He snaked an arm about her hips and pulled her closer and cupped a breast with the other hand. Again, his wife murmured something in her sleep. She curled her body into his, her limbs pliant, her lips soft and welcoming.

For a woman who was most definitely not in his usual style, he enjoyed kissing her. That mouth alone held a lifetime of secrets, and oddly, the not knowing them piqued his curiosity when he hadn't had that in a bed partner for a very long time indeed.

The second he brushed the pad of his thumb over her nipple and brought it into a tight bud, she stirred, whispered a garbled noise, a sound of invitation perhaps. He paused, wondering what was going on inside her head, pondered also her history with her first husband. Murky hints about him bobbed to the surface of the muck of his memory, but he suspected she'd suffered greatly.

The warmth of her beckoned, as did the lush welcome of her lips.

Again, he kissed her, and after a few seconds, she responded, returned the overture with a decent skill and a surprising ardor. Daring much, he teased the seam of her lips with his tongue until she opened for him, and when their tongues met and electric lust leapt between them, he worried that nipple once more, for her full breast was a pleasant weight in his palm.

Damn if he couldn't wait to tease that flesh, taste it.

Up through the obscurity of his thoughts bubbled the little niggle of a rumor that this woman had allegedly killed her first husband.

No sooner had he paused in his erotic ministrations than her eyes flew open. Shock clouded those brown depths. She gasped, sat up so quickly in the bed that the points of her aroused nipples showed through her shift. Then she raised a hand and slapped him so hard his cheek stung from the impact.

The cat, jerked from sleep by the noise, jumped to the floor and ran into the adjoining dressing room.

"How dare you attempt to molest me!" Her mouth worked but no sound came out, but fury sparked in her eyes and her hand shook as she raised it a second time. "Touched me without my consent."

Surprise wrenched him from thoughts of carnal activity. Montague struggled into a sitting position as she scrambled from the bed. Yes, they were wed and under current law, she was his wife and had certain duties toward him, but never in his life had he taken a woman against her will. It wasn't his plan to start now.

Hot words of anger rested on the tip of his tongue, his head pounded in time to the pain in his cheek, yet… she had a point. With a sigh, he pushed a hand through his hair. "I apologize." Tousled from sleep but with eyes snapping in fury, something about her drew his attention. Against his better judgment. "When I awoke, disoriented, I—"

"—lost your mind?" She propped her hands on the curve of her hips, which only directed his focus to the lower portion of her anatomy. "Since your brain isn't quite as pickled as it might have been last night, let me remind you that being wed does not give you control over my body."

Had she been so *loud* yesterday? The pain in his head increased. "I realize that." Who was she to dictate anything to him? He grabbed hold of his ever-present anger and kept it in the forefront.

"Yet each time I've been in your company, you've shown me you are nothing more than a beast, intent on catering to your vices."

What the devil? "I've hardly spent time in your company."

"Exactly, and yet I have a truly poor opinion of you. I wonder how that came to pass." Sarcasm fairly dripped from her words.

He glared. "Then I must have imagined your enthusiasm while kissing me back."

A trace of pink went across her cheeks. "Obviously, I wasn't aware of my actions."

"Right." While her chest heaved and he continued to regard her with annoyance, charged tension fairly crackled between them. Out of all the women in London, how had he been forced into marriage with the most impossible, a woman who set his teeth on edge? "Once I've indulged in morning ablutions and perhaps taken breakfast, you and I need to talk, to clarify expectations within this union." The words came out around a growl.

"Fine. In the meanwhile, you can leave this room." She pointed at the door, and when he apparently didn't move fast enough, she huffed, came forward, pushed at his chest, and kept shoving until he walked backward toward the door. "This is *my* apartment; I demand you respect my space since this is where I will reside unless I absolutely must suffer through your company until other arrangements can be made."

As if I'm the one in the wrong!

Neither of his fiancées had been this contrary or strident. They had both been the epitome of genteel grace and proper society perfection, suitable to the position of countess. Not this, this… harridan. And why the hell couldn't he stop staring at her lips? He fumbled at the door latch. "Why must you prove the shrew?"

"Why must you give me just cause to be so?"

"Damn it, woman, stop arguing!"

"Argh!" With one final shove, she pushed him out into the corridor, then she slammed the door in his face.

Well, if she assumed he would always act the beast, then that's what she would see from him. The first thing he would do today before meeting with his disagreeable wife was confront the owner of the Lyon's Den, since this whole mess could be laid squarely at her feet.

MONTAGUE DIDN'T ARRIVE at the gaming hell until two o'clock that afternoon, but business was as brisk as it usually was.

The first person he encountered upon stepping into the main gaming floor was one of the women who acted as security agents. The statuesque blonde lifted an eyebrow when she caught sight of him. Had she been warned he might make an appearance? Regardless, he couldn't remember her name, only that it was from a Shakespearean play.

"I require an audience with Mrs. Dove-Lyon immediately," he said before she could send him away. "I'm afraid it cannot wait."

"I am sorry, Lord Pennington, but Mrs. Dove-Lyon is indisposed at the moment. Her schedule is quite full."

"To be honest, I don't care about that." He shoved the brim of his beaver felt top hat higher on his forehead. "Mrs. Dove-Lyon was the person who mucked about in my life, and she's the reason I have an angry and quite petite dervish ensconced in my townhouse at this moment." He glared at the guardian of the gaming floor, uncaring that his voice had risen and that more than a few patrons looked his way. "I demand an audience, and if it makes a difference, I'm not going away until that happens."

The woman's lips twitched. Amusement danced in her dark eyes. "Gentlemen are not allowed to loiter on the floor. They must join a game or move on."

"Then show me upstairs to talk with your damned mistress!"

She sighed. "Follow me, Lord Pennington. No doubt our hostess already knows of your… distress."

The trip through the corridors was familiar since he was shown the way the day he'd won the baron's daughter at the gaming table. Once more, he was ushered into the same room where he'd talked to the owner of this establishment. The attendant went into the adjoining room, which he assumed was a dressing or reception room of sorts. The low murmur of voices buzzed in the air for a few minutes, then the attendant returned, beckoning him into that area.

"Her time is limited, so make your case quickly, for then you must leave. I'll wait here at the door."

Ah, he wasn't allowed access to full privacy this time around. "Thank you." At least he was given this boon. After dismissing the blonde from his mind, he came further into the room that was lit with the afternoon sunlight streaming in through the windows draped with elegant and quite expensive silk and velvet curtains in a vibrant turquoise hue. "Mrs. Dove-Lyon?" He couldn't immediately discern the woman.

A sigh issued from behind a silk privacy screen at one side of the room. Flowers and leaves in an Oriental style had been painted upon the silk. "I must say I'm surprised to find you here at the Lyon's Den so soon into your marriage, Lord Pennington." The rustle of fabric indicated she was changing clothes. "I thought you would perhaps involve yourself in honeymoon activities."

Was the woman that daft? Surely she knew there was no love present in the union.

"I rather think the mess I've landed in doesn't deserve a honeymoon," he spat out. "After all, what is there to celebrate?" And bedding a woman full of prickles didn't inspire desire.

For long moments, the sound of rustling taffeta met his ears. Quiet direction from what he assumed was a maid echoed in the sudden silence. Finally, Mrs. Dove-Lyon spoke again. "You've bedded women for less in the past. Are you not pleased with your wife?"

"What do you think?" When she didn't answer, he shook his head in disbelief. "You duped me, plain and simple. Routed me lock, stock, and artillery, by switching out my intended bride with a woman much older and steeped in scandal."

To say nothing of possessing a wicked temper and a decent aim in her slap.

"There is nothing I can do about that, Your Lordship. Mrs. Roberts, or perhaps I should call her Lady Pennington now, presented me with a compelling offer, so I let her go ahead in her sister's place."

So, what the woman had told him last night was the truth. *Well, damn.*

"I don't want her." Truth be told, he didn't want either of them, didn't want the marriage or the hassle that went along with it. "She cannot bear children. What is the point?"

He didn't want to allow hope into his life only to reap disappointment.

"I rather think that is not an issue up for debate. The deed is done." Once more, fabric rustled, followed by the unmistakable sound of a perfume pump being deployed. Immediately, the mysterious scents of flowers, amber, and musk were buoyed through the air. "Since I am not the head of the church, I cannot have the marriage annulled, and if I wagered coin on it, you don't wish to go to the time nor vast expense in the pursuit of such. Your reputation and hers being what they are."

Montague gritted his teeth. "Of course not." It would destroy all facets of his life, and quite frankly, after the snatches of what he'd gleaned about his wife, Adriana didn't deserve that.

Metallic bracelets clinked together. "Then my best advice to you is this. Play the hand you've been dealt, Lord Pennington. Play it to the best of your ability, even if you are forced to bluff your way through at times."

"And then what?" Was that all there was, then? He had no recourse but to go back to his house and find common ground with his wife? "I rather think we don't have a future." How could they?

"That isn't for me to say, Your Lordship."

A giggle emanated from the maid.

A stab of anger went through his chest. Did no one care about his plight? "One more question, Mrs. Dove-Lyon. Do you particularly enjoy destroying the lives of the people around you? Are you that devious?"

"That was two questions, Lord Pennington." Her tone was droll. "However, I don't think of what I do as destruction. I consider it more of a reset or a chance to reorder misfortune into what it should have been all along."

"You, madam, are *quite* impossible." He pivoted on his heel and strode to the door.

"Any woman worth her salt is, Your Lordship. Remember that," Mrs. Dove-Lyon called after him with clear amusement hanging from the words.

"Damn fool women," he muttered to the blonde attendant as she showed him out of the suite and back into the corridor. "I will shake the dust of this place from my boots and will never darken the doorways of the Lyon's Den again."

"I shall relay your message to Mrs. Dove-Lyon. I am sure she'll make your preference known downstairs so the men may wager upon whether your word will be kept or not."

Dear God, save me from the troublesome females who inhabit this place.

AN HOUR LATER, Montague returned to his townhouse, in a fouler mood than when he left it. If everyone thought his life was a game, then they'd given him no choice but to play along. His countess had wished for this, so now she would reap all of those rewards. He intended to make her life as miserable as possible, and in that way perhaps her pain and anguish would match his.

Finally tracking her to the morning room, he slammed open the door so hard that the panel crashed against the wall. The echoes of that reverberated through the air. "A word, if you please, Lady Pennington."

She'd startled at his entrance but kept her seat behind a small secretary where she'd been writing letters. The dull gray day dress she'd donned did nothing to put life into her cheeks or eyes, and it was woefully out of style besides. How could she conduct herself as his countess if she didn't know the first thing about fashion?

"Of course, Your Lordship."

"Pennington."

"What?" Confusion lined her expression.

"Refer to me as Pennington or even Montague. It matters not, but you will *not* assume a role as less than me. You are a countess. Comport yourself as such." If he couldn't escape the marriage, then by God he would play the game to the hilt.

"Fine." Twin spots of high color blazed in her previously pale cheeks as she slowly rose to her feet. "What would you say to me, *Pennington*?" Frost had formed in her voice and glittered in the dark brown depths of her eyes.

The title didn't sit as well with him as he'd assumed, but he would puzzle out the whys later. "Since our union is legal in the eyes of the law and church, there is naught that we can do but see it through to the bitter end."

"Ah, then you intend to murder me in my bed?" Once more, sarcasm accompanied the question.

Damn, but he had the powerful urge to kiss that arched eyebrow. Why? They were nothing but enemies, correct? "Not unless *you* kill *me* first, since you are the one with the experience." That wasn't well done of him, but he couldn't recall the words now. For whatever reason, being in the vicinity of this woman sent his dander and his ire surging.

She narrowed her eyes, but not before a trace of hurt clouded those dark depths. "Then it would behoove you to mind yourself around me."

Did that mean she was guilty?

Not knowing, he cleared his throat. "Here are the terms of our nuptial life, and might I preface it with this. Do not expect love or affection from me. I simply do not have that to give. Not anymore." He paused, his jaw working. "However, the undeniable fact is I am not growing younger; neither are you. At some point soon, I shall require an heir, so physical contact will need to happen."

More hurt clouded her eyes. "I told you last night I cannot conceive a child."

That remained to be seen, for there could have been too many issues regarding her husband and their circumstances to make such a thing possible. "Until I am certain of that myself, we will assume this isn't so."

Desolation mixed with an odd flare of hope in those expressive eyes, and it tugged at his compassion. "Ah, then so I should welcome you into my bed, let you rut and impregnate me, without giving thought to my pleasure?" She crossed her arms beneath her breasts, and for a few seconds, his gaze dipped to her bodice where the tops of those charms barely peeked out.

Did she retreat into disagreement as a way to protect herself? Another thing he would need to discover. "When I bed a woman, she is well pleasured indeed."

Why the hell had he said *that*? Was he teasing her or trying to entice her?

Surprise jumped into her face, followed by another blush. "Ah."

Dear God, had her bounder of a husband never sent her over the edge? How… intriguing. "Let us both pray you are fertile and getting you *enceinte* will occur quickly." The last thing he wanted was to share the ultimate intimacy with the woman who'd duped him at the altar, even if the possibility of introducing her to the wonders therein was quite tempting. Yet… why couldn't he fathom bedding her like he'd done mistresses in the past? Her form wasn't so bad…

Focus, Pennington. She is not your type.

"Agreed. And the next item? For once *that* task is accomplished, we shall have no need to be around each other." She gave no quarter.

For that she had his respect. This would have gone much more badly had she wilted and sought refuge in tears. "There shall be no contact with your family for the first three months of our union. I don't want them mucking about or trying to manipulate you."

"That is quite fine with me. I have nothing to say to them at this point." She shrugged, and again, his gaze tumbled to her bodice. "If they don't care then I don't."

Interesting. "You won't have contact with your friends either."

"I haven't any. They left long ago when scandal hit." A hint of vulnerability went over her face, and damn his eyes, he wished to know why.

This wasn't going at all how he'd hoped. "There will be no leaving the townhouse unless you are accompanied by me or one of the upper servants."

Her lips formed a tight line of annoyance. "Where would I go? I'm not accepted into bastions of *ton* excellence like Almack's, and the only place where I've ever felt comfortable is Hyde Park." She shrugged. "My governess used to take me there when I was a child, and sometimes when things were… difficult in my marriage, I sought refuge…" Her words trailed off and she gasped, as if she couldn't quite believe she'd shared so much with him.

It only made him more curious about her.

Damn woman! "You will take dinner with me every night to maintain an image of a proper *ton* marriage."

She snorted. "Ah, then showing your friends and members of parliament that you aren't keeping your wife a veritable prisoner *isn't* a good idea?" The tone was sweet enough, but her eyes shot daggers at him.

"You are not a prisoner."

"Ha. It sounds like I am."

"How you choose to interpret the rules is not my concern, and perhaps you should have considered that before you switched places with your sister." He glared. "You will make appearances in society with me, so please have a modiste in so that you might have a proper wardrobe."

"Fine." Annoyance crossed her face.

"And lastly, my suite of rooms as well as the library is off limits to you. Those are *my* private areas, and I don't wish them disturbed."

A spark of curiosity briefly lit her face. "I suppose I should have expected such high-handed treatment and overt arrogance." She stalked around him to the door. "After all, I haven't had any sort of choice in my life until this point. Why should you extend me any sort of trust or different treatment?" The withering glance she gave him twisted through his chest like hot knives. "If that is the gauntlet you've thrown down, don't be surprised when I retaliate with one of my own. Enjoy your tea, Pennington."

Then she swept out of the room with her chin held high, and for whatever reason, her righteous indignation tugged a grin from him.

It was rather amusing to needle her. He hadn't felt exhilarated like that in a very long time indeed. What the hell was wrong with him?

CHAPTER SIX

October 16, 1817

O NE FULL DAY after her husband had laid down expectations—*his* expectations—for their union, Adriana still seethed with anger.

How dare he dictate to her how she should live her life? Especially when he hadn't the common courtesy to talk to her as if she'd mattered. There'd been no civilized conversation, no give or take with questions or how she felt about this major shift in life. He'd merely snapped and snarled at her, demanded that she give in to his rules.

Well, he will soon see I am not the type of woman to roll over and give in.

Not a second time around.

The key to finding common ground and peace in their union was understanding the man she'd married, the man beyond the rumors. If she didn't wish for him to judge her for the same, she owed it to them both to delve deeper. Perhaps if he could pull himself out of the vices he used to keep reality at bay, he might give her the same courtesy.

And the quickest way to do that was to befriend the staff.

As she dabbed the corners of her mouth with a linen napkin and looked at the detritus of the tea she'd completed, Adriana smiled at the butler. "How long have you been with the earl, Pearson?" Every so often, she would pet the black cat that had poked his way into the room as soon as she'd occupied it. Apparently comfortable around her, Satan had jumped into her lap and had gone right to sleep.

The middle-aged man, perhaps several years older than Lord Pennington, paused in the task of gathering the used dishes to glance at her with surprise. "Well, let me think." He straightened to his full height; he was quite a tall man. "The current earl took the title nearly twenty years ago when his father died in a riding accident." With the tap of a long finger to his chin, he continued. "I came into his employ eight years before this one, after he lost Lady Catherine."

"His sister?" Truly, she had no idea about the earl's personal history.

"No, Your Ladyship, his first fiancée." He continued to gather the tea things onto a silver tray. "He was devastated upon her death, wished for a change in his life, so he fired all the servants his father had employed, with the exception of the cook and Mrs. Beacon the housekeeper. She hired a whole new staff."

"Oh." Adriana couldn't imagine Pennington having the capacity for soft feelings or even unbending enough to give his heart to anyone. "What of his mother?"

The butler shrugged. "From what I understand, she died during childbirth when the earl was a young boy."

Well, that took care of her next question regarding siblings. Adriana rose to her feet, dislodging Satan in the process. He told her of his annoyance and then took up residence beneath the table. "Does he, ah, currently keep a mistress?" Heat fired in her cheeks, but even her family, with as limited access to the *haute ton* as they had, knew the rumors about the worst man in London.

"I wouldn't know, Your Ladyship." There was no censure in his voice or expression, only a trace of pity.

She didn't want that. *I made this decision. It's time to make it work for me.* "What is the name of his valet?"

"Tremaine. Michael Tremaine."

"Thank you, Pearson. I appreciate the insight, and I shall be certain to introduce myself to him." She would talk with that man soon.

As the butler picked up the tea tray, he cast a furtive glance to the door then found her gaze with his. "Lord Pennington wasn't always so disagreeable," he said in a low voice. "From what I understand of him before… misfortune hit, he was quite affable."

Adriana snorted. "I'll have to take your word for that."

"Grief pulls a man in many directions and can take many forms. Please don't hold that against him." With a nod, he left the room on swift feet.

No sooner did she gain the doorway when she encountered the earl himself, and his expression resembled a thundercloud.

What would he look like if he grinned? She couldn't imagine. "Good afternoon, Pennington."

He scowled. "Why were you talking with Pearson?"

Was he mad? "Why wouldn't I? He is part of the staff here at Bassage House, and since I reside beneath the roof as well, I wished to begin a relationship."

"I won't have anyone indulging in gossip." Pennington chopped the air with a hand. "Do you understand?" The scent of his shaving soap wafted to her nose. Why did he have to smell good as well as look so sinfully handsome? If he were an ugly, stinky man, his prickly attitude might be tolerated slightly better.

She refrained from huffing in frustration. "It wasn't gossip. I merely wished to discover more about you and your history." He was the type of man who wouldn't tolerate pity, and in that she completely agreed, but it wouldn't hurt to offer understanding. "And treating the people who work for you nicely goes a long way."

"I don't want you mucking about in household matters. Everyone has their duties." A warning growled through the deep timbre of his voice.

Annoyance stabbed through her chest. Must he be so disagreeable *all* the time? Yet, he certainly hadn't been yesterday morning when he'd kissed her when she hadn't yet come fully out of sleep. When she had enjoyed that bit of intimacy they'd shared despite him going about it the wrong way. *Stop thinking about him like that!* Heat slapped at her cheeks. Though she'd kissed him back for the same reasons, it had meant nothing beyond curiosity, yet in those kisses, there had been a hint, a glimmer of everything she hadn't had with her first husband. "That very well be true. However, you have been quite rude toward me and have neglected to introduce me to the staff, so I am doing that myself. As is my right as your countess."

"So, this is my fault?"

"Absolutely, it is." As much as she wished to poke a forefinger into his chest, she quelled the urge. "You are going out of your way to play the beast; I don't appreciate it."

A muscle in his cheek ticced, for he'd no doubt clenched his teeth. "I shall discuss matters with you at dinner tonight."

She shook her head. "Speak with me now, Pennington. At least give me that respect as your wife. You've done your best to avoid me all day." In fact, she hadn't seen him since dinner last night. Had he been licking his wounds, or did he truly not care?

Worse yet, had he spent the night with a mistress? It didn't matter that what they shared was a marriage of convenience with a hearty dose of raw awareness, she would demand his fidelity if he wished for an heir down the line.

"I have business yet this afternoon." Without saying goodbye, he stepped around her and continued along the corridor toward the stairs.

"Oh, he is so… so… exasperating!" And he hadn't alleviated the need to discover more about him. In fact, with every unproductive meeting, more questions popped into her mind like soap bubbles.

What to do?

Start at the beginning, and that meant going into the lair of the beast himself. After taking a few deep breaths and releasing them to calm her racing heart, Adriana followed the corridor and then lightly ran up the stairs to the next level. The soles of her slippers provided barely a whisper and the skirts of her lightweight wool day dress in boring brown rubbed against her legs.

When she reached the door to his suite, she pressed the brass handle and pushed open the panel. The bedchamber was empty, and she hoped that meant the valet had gone down to the servants' hall for his own tea, so she could poke about undetected.

After closing the door behind her, Adriana stepped more fully into the bedroom. Why the devil hadn't the draperies been opened? It gave the room a dreary, gloomy atmosphere. With a huff, she crossed the plush Aubusson carpeting done in shades of navy and gray, then at the first window, she flung open the heavy curtains. Late afternoon sunlight flooded the space, and she did the same with the second window.

"That's better." She glanced about the space. The apartment had been tastefully decorated with the same colors in the carpet; all furniture was of heavy, dark cherry wood—a large four-poster bed, a low bureau, a curio cabinet in one corner, a few small round tables, and a comfortable-looking winged-back chair where a stack of books waited on a nearby table beneath a candle in a brass holder.

The whole space smelled like him: cedar, citrus, and spices. The bedclothes were still rumpled, so obviously he didn't let the maids in here often. When she peeked into the adjoining dressing room, it had the same dark theme, except paintings of all sorts leaned against the walls. Portraits of women who were beautiful yet of the same coloring. A glance about the bedchamber showed the same, all resting against the far wall.

Adriana padded over to them. A few of the women in the portraits were nude, but the skill of the artist had captured them in such a way it was almost as if the subjects of the paintings were living and breathing, as if she could reach out and touch them through the canvas. Two of the portraits had a large, red slash mark over the faces.

Why? What was it about those women either the artist, or the earl, didn't like?

With even more questions than answers, she moved to his bed, glanced at the indentation on a pillow. Just the one, which meant he hadn't had a mistress with him. That only brought a modicum of relief. A bottle of brandy rested on the bedside table along with a cut-crystal tumbler with a trace of the amber liquid still inside. Frowning, she tugged open the table drawer.

A few more books met her eyes, a handkerchief, a thin, rectangular box containing sheaths, another bottle of brandy, and at the bottom were two separate stacks of yellowed letters. One was tied with a blue satin ribbon; the other bound by yellow.

After making certain the door remained closed, she brought one of the stacks out, tugged the top one from the stack, and then quickly unfolded the letter, obviously the most recent of the set. Written eight years ago. Flowery writing covered the page, and as she skimmed the contents, she quickly ascertained it had been written by a fiancée, Catherine—his first. It was full of breezy news and anecdotal stories about the writer. At the end, she'd told Pennington how much she loved him and couldn't wait to marry him.

Oh, dear. This felt too much like prying, but she couldn't stop. After replacing the letter and putting the stack back into the drawer, she did the same with the other set.

The most recent one had been written three years before, and read along the same lines at the other she'd read. From his second fiancée—Rachel—she too couldn't wait to marry him—the date was but a week off from the date of the letter, apparently—had loved him to distraction and had gushed over her excitement of being his wife, of starting a family with him.

From the clues she'd included in the letter and a conversation she referred back to that had happened between her and the earl, it seemed the woman was nearly three months along with child.

Oh, God.

He must have been devastated.

Twice.

Had he looked forward to that baby? No wonder he'd appeared shocked and a bit shattered when Adriana had informed him of her inability to conceive.

Tears prickled the backs of her eyelids. Her hands shook as she replaced the letter in its stack and gently rested the packet into the drawer. Pennington had been engaged twice, and twice something had occurred to prevent him from wedding.

But what and why?

She quietly closed the drawer. Was that what had sent him into a spiral, that plunged him into the vices? Was being the worst man in London just a façade to hide a shredded and aching heart drowning in grief? Perhaps the anger was but another outlet or even a screen for that.

But she wouldn't know for certain until she spoke with him, encouraged him to tell her those secrets. Would he trust her enough for that? To that end, did she trust him enough to put in the time in order to draw him out? Because if she were to perhaps help him through his anger, his grief, his disappointment, she would need to reveal hers as well, and life—men—had shown her time and time again they weren't to be trusted.

At all.

A sticky wicket indeed.

As idea filled her mind, Adriana padded into the dressing room. Somehow, Satan had found her even here. He jumped into a window-sill and then proceeded to ignore her. She glanced at the washstand and basin in one corner, noted another stack of books resting near a chair by a window with curtains drawn, wandered over to a clothes-press with exquisite carvings of birds and woodland animals in the doors. When she tugged open one of the panels and regarded the jackets hanging in orderly fashion within, she breathed deeply of his scent that was becoming all too familiar.

What did he do in his leisure time besides reading? For a man who didn't care for that wouldn't have stacks of books in every room he occupied. And why did he have so many paintings throughout his suite? Was he an enthusiast of the women depicted there or of the artist?

Much like his suite of rooms, her husband needed to let the light into his soul. As she yanked open the drapes at the window, the door to the corridor swung open. With a gasp, Adriana spun about. Pennington stood in the frame, and when his gaze landed on her, fury lined his face. Anger brewed in the blue-gray depths of his eyes.

In that moment, with the sunlight hitting him just so, he was mag-nificent in his ire.

"What the hell are you doing in here?" He came into the room and slammed the door behind him.

"I… I…" Why wouldn't the words come out? She took one look at the cat, who scampered to the floor and then out into the adjoining room. "You said you had business."

"I decided to postpone it." He took slow stalking steps toward her. "I warned you from this suite. Of course, you couldn't possibly follow orders. Could you?"

Finally, her tongue became unstuck. "I follow orders perfectly well when they aren't arbitrary and make no sense."

"This isn't up for debate!" His roar of anger echoed off the wall. "I won't be disobeyed in my own house by my own wife." Before she could speak or take a step, he strode across the floor, closed the distance, then his large hands were on her shoulders. He shuttled her across the floor until her back connected against the wall.

"Must you act the beast every time I see you?" Despite her racing heartbeat and the fear that twisted down her spine, she lifted her chin. If he accosted her, she had no qualms about jamming a knee into the soft flesh between his legs. When she went to edge around him, he planted a palm on the wall at the side of her head, leaned into her, blocking her escape. The clothespress stood at her other side and neatly boxed her in.

"Explain." The one-word demand sent a wash of tingling awareness over her skin. The power he exuded was all-consuming, and oh so tempting.

What would it feel like to let him rage about her and to give up control to him for a little while?

"I…" Her swallow was audible, and she had no choice except to glare up at him. "I wished to know you better by investigating the places where you spend the most time."

"Even after I expressly forbid it?"

"Yes, especially because of that since you refuse to act civilly toward me." Sexual tension fairly crackled between them. His big presence filled the room, and she was all too aware of him as a man, as her husband. Need awakened in places she thought long dormant. Heat emanated from him in waves. He was darkly beautiful in the afternoon light, and the pain behind the fury in his eyes tugged at her, beckoned to her, picked at her own. "What other recourse did I have?"

"None. You have none, but you knew that when you married me in your sister's place, didn't you?" A growl rumbled in the low-pitched words. "However, you shouldn't be here. This is my sanctuary, a place where women don't belong."

What a load of rubbish. "I am your wife! That allows me access to all of you."

The earl leaned farther into her, trapping her between him and the wall. "I'm your husband, yet you don't seem to remember that."

Tingles moved through her belly, of anticipation or fear, she couldn't say. "You shouldn't keep secrets. We are married."

He snorted. "That doesn't matter."

Oh, so he would be difficult even now? "Like hell it doesn't." She poked at his chest with her forefinger, his hard, warm chest, and she well remembered what his form had felt like pressed to hers yesterday morning when he'd kissed her. "I… I demand you respect me. That means talking to me," she said in a hushed voice as her gaze went to his sensual mouth. "I refuse to have you think I'm your plaything only or that you assume my permission doesn't matter." When he would have protested, she poked him again. "Regardless of whether or not I enjoyed certain… things."

And drat her if she didn't need to feel him against her again.

"Yet you cannot do the same for me." His eyes darkened, and it was the most marvelous thing she'd ever seen, like a storm moving across the land.

With a little shake of her head, she held onto her anger. "That's not the same! You have to give in order to receive something in exchange." Her breath came in tiny pants. Being in such close proximity to him, feeling the banked energy of him inflamed her own.

Surely, she didn't desire him so fiercely? Never had that happened before.

"Why should I? Nothing is permanent, and perhaps I am too far gone for anything like that now." With his free hand, he snaked his fingers about her nape and dragged her to him. "I *am* the worst man in London for a reason."

Adriana trembled, from his touch or his words. "I suspect it's for protection, a—"

With a growl, he claimed her mouth in a hard kiss no doubt de-signed to punish, to stem her words, perhaps to frighten her, but she was made of much sterner stuff than that.

And yes, she had kissed him back yesterday morning for the sheer pleasure of it. During the course of her first marriage, she'd had precious little of that, and she enjoyed the act of kissing. It was no less wonderful now, except in a raw, big, hot, consuming way. She slid her hands up his chest, curved her fingers into his lapels, and returned his overture with as much passion, desire, wounded emotion that he'd given her.

For the space of a few heartbeats, they warred for dominance, then Pennington softened the kiss, made love to her mouth as if it were the most natural thing in the world, made her feel almost… cherished.

But that was silly, wasn't it?

With a tiny sound of surrender, Adriana melted into him without a shred of shame. She looped her arms about his shoulders while he pressed her body into the wall, trapped her between it and his large frame, pressed himself so intimately to her that there was no mistaking the desire he felt for her. Over and over, he drank from her, and when he encouraged her lips apart, sought out her tongue with his, she was lost on the sheer primal connection of it.

Seconds, minutes, hours later, he abruptly released her, and she sagged against the wall.

"Get out, Lady Pennington." He shoved a hand through his hair, upsetting it into furrowed rows. Shock reflected in his eyes. "I cannot do this again."

What, exactly, did "this" refer to?

"But I thought we—"

"I said get out!" The thunderous roar echoed off the walls and hurt her ears.

Without another word, Adriana fled the room, leaving the door gaping open behind her. She didn't stop running until she'd gained the first level of the townhouse, and with her heartbeat hammering like rapid fire behind her ribcage, she shakily asked Pearson to have a carriage brought around for her.

Old habits, and perhaps older terrors, came home to roost. His behavior was outside of enough, and it was frightening, for she knew how that tale would end. Regardless of his skill in kissing, raw carnality wouldn't be able to save her from possible abuse or a lifetime of living in fear... of being alone and trapped in a loveless marriage.

Eventually, she directed the carriage driver to take her to Hyde Park. It was the only place she could think of that would give her the privacy to sort through her thoughts and compose herself. The man she'd wed was an ogre. Unless he let her past his thorny exterior, their marriage would never work.

Did she want it to?

At the moment, she had no answers, but she had already survived a horrid union; she damn well wouldn't let this one follow the same path. If that meant standing up to him, defying him at every turn, not backing down until they came to an understanding, so be it.

Something had to give. This time, it wouldn't be her.

CHAPTER SEVEN

MONTAGUE'S WHOLE LIFE was shifting beneath his feet. Where once he was content enough to hide behind his anger and grief—and Adriana had been quite right to categorize it as hiding—cracks had begun to make their jagged way through that wall he'd built around himself.

Why?

Because of the advent of one petite storm who refused to follow orders and leave well enough alone. A woman with enough curves to tempt St. Peter while leaving St. Paul with a cockstand. The termagant who he'd taken to wife by accident on his part and design on hers.

"Argh!" In a moment of weakness, he'd kissed the hell out of his wife, but the emotion that had spurred the embrace had been frustration and anger, and yes, full-on lust, for he hadn't been able to evict the woman from his mind since that kiss in her bed yesterday morning. "But it cannot happen again," he told the clothespress that still gaped open from her intrusion. "That kiss was motivated by pure annoyance. Nothing more," he assured an occasional table as he strode to the window and closed the draperies.

Why couldn't she leave well enough alone?

Why couldn't she leave *him* alone?

That's what he wanted, wasn't it? To be left alone, just as he had been for the past three years? The last time his world had shifted.

Except, every time he was in Adriana's company, he felt different, almost as a wind of change was blowing over him. When she challenged him, picked at the threads that held him together, he was both terrified and… hopeful.

For what?

He didn't wish to answer that question or delve into the reasons why. Instead, he slammed out of the room and strode along the corridor. At the stairs, he raced down them, his feet barely touching each tread, and he didn't stop until he gained the main floor.

"Pearson! Where the devil are you, man?"

A few seconds later, the butler came running down the corridor, winded, and with worry clearly in his expression. "Is something amiss, Your Lordship?"

That all depended on one's perspective. Ironic, that. "I'm not certain. Where is Lady Pennington?" If anyone knew, it would be the butler.

"I put her into your carriage not twenty minutes past." Pearson frowned. "She was visibly upset but waved me off when I inquired."

Well, damn. She hadn't let him see that he'd affected her. His respect continued to grow. "Do you know her direction?"

"I do not."

Montague's stomach bottomed out. Did that mean she'd left him? Where would she go and without packing her belongings? From the way she'd spoken about her family, she wouldn't return to them. He frowned as he propped his hands on his hips. "Where the devil is she headed?"

"I couldn't say, Your Lordship. She sent the carriage back. Charles from the mews said it was empty." Pearson peered at him with speculation. "Did the two of you have another row?"

Heat went up the back of his neck. "More or less. It seems we got on like oil and water just now."

"If I may offer a few words of encouragement?"

It couldn't hurt. "Of course."

"On the surface, oil and water will never blend, but if one shakes them up and adds a few spices, they become a rather enjoyable addition to salad greens. On their own, oil and water could never accomplish that, but according to Cook, spice is the key to any successful recipe."

"Thank you, Pearson. I shall bear that in mind." He rubbed a hand along the side of his face. Perhaps he and his wife had spice enough. Hadn't that kiss shown him that? It had been years since he'd felt that sort of passion for a woman. Had it been desperation on her part or lust on his that made them come together like that? Who could say, but now they needed to find a way to blend their oil and water sides.

If such a thing were possible.

If they both wished for a harmonious union.

Yet I cannot give her my heart or even my love. I'm not strong enough to withstand that aftermath.

"Ah, Pearson, could you please have my carriage brought 'round and request that Charles drive it?"

"Of course, Your Lordship." Pearson pressed a gloved fingertip to the side of his nose, and then spoke again. "Will you bring Lady Pennington back home?"

"Do *you* think I should?" For the first time since he'd brought the man onto his staff, he valued the man's opinion.

"I do." He nodded. "You see, it's been rather nice having a lady in residence. Almost cheerful, even if we don't know her well yet." The butler shrugged. "Additionally, she is not afraid to stand toe to toe with you. Such a woman deserves respect. From us all."

"That she does." Perhaps he *had* gone out of his way to antagonize her, but he couldn't quite tame the beast inside because he *was* wounded, lost to grief, and couldn't see a way out. "I shall need my greatcoat as well. There is a decided nip in the air." And he might have a terrible time of locating his wife.

AFTER CHARLES DROVE the vehicle to the location where he'd dropped Adriana off, Montague asked that he linger, for he intended to escort his wife home, but as he threw a glance about the area around the entrance, the muscles in his belly clenched. Hyde Park wasn't his favorite place in London to visit, not after what happened eight years ago to his first fiancée.

So, of course, that was where his wife had run to. Even in this, when she knew absolutely nothing of his history, she would antagonize him, challenge him to face his fears.

Bloody hell.

Perhaps that was what Mrs. Dove-Lyon meant when she'd said to play the hand he'd been dealt. Had she had an inkling ahead of time that Adriana might prove the catalyst he needed? There was no way to tell.

Nestling deeper into his greatcoat, he set out down one of the paths in search of his wayward wife.

A half hour later, as the sun began its descent and covered the area with the purpling shadows of near twilight, he finally came upon her near one of the Serpentine's curves. But she wasn't alone. While she sat upon a moss-covered stone bench half-hidden by shrubbery, a tall man stood nearby, mousy looking, retiring, and from all accounts, proper with manners, for he wasn't attempting to molest or bother her. From their relaxed body language, it would appear they knew each other prior.

Still, jealousy stabbed through his chest, and he unashamedly eavesdropped on their conversation from his position on the path.

Their backs were to him, and as of yet, neither of them had noticed him.

"How have you been keeping yourself, Mrs. Roberts, er, I meant, Lady Pennington?" the man asked, his tone pleasant and solicitous.

"Well enough." Her answer was so low, Montague could barely hear it.

The man shifted his weight from foot to foot. "I worry because you are married to that monster, the worst man in London. The man has had dozens of mistresses and members of the demimonde in his bed." He scoffed. "Lord Pennington doesn't deserve you, Adriana."

Montague bristled. No one had the right to call *his* wife by her Christian name.

"Whether he does or does not, I *am* married to him." Emotion graveled her voice, and when she glanced up at him, he caught her face in profile. The slope of her cheeks, the round chin, the tendrils of blonde hair that clung to the side of her neck were all softened in the fading light. In that moment, she resembled a master's dream and should be immortalized on canvas, a true Raphaelite's subject.

His fingers itched to take up his own brushes. Could he find the right mix of paints to capture the myriad of blondes in her hair?

"Lord Pennington is my husband. I shall muddle through because nothing is as bad as what I had before."

Montague pressed a hand to his chest. Did she truly think him as bad—or worse—than her previous husband? For the first time he regretted what he'd made himself into as a matter of self-preservation.

"You shouldn't have to muddle through." The fervent note in the man's voice recalled Montague from his musings. Then the pup had the audacity to rest a hand on her shoulder. "You should have a man who adores you, a man who would pray to God every night with gratitude that he has you at his side."

"Oh, Richard." She trained her gaze onto the river. "You are indeed a gallant man."

Montague clenched his jaw. This was outside of enough! But before he could run the younger man off, Adriana spoke again.

"I am certain you will make some lady a fine husband. However, I am not that woman, and now that I *am* wed, I must ask that you not seek me out when alone. It's not proper."

"But I can take you away from him! Treat you like a queen."

A sigh escaped her. "I've turned you down even before I wed the earl."

"Yes, but now it's imperative you take me seriously."

Adriana shook her head. "It's not to be, so I shall ask you again. Please go. If Pennington were to catch us together, there will be hell to pay, and quite frankly, I am exhausted from arguing just now."

The emotion in her voice tugged at his chest. Damn his own eyes for acting the arse.

"Of course I will go, but I will never give up on you or freeing you from that monster."

"Do stop. In some ways, I rather think this union was fated to happen. Perhaps it was one of those things that when thought of too many times eventually came to pass, but not in the way I had hoped."

What the devil did that mean?

"You are far better than him." He leaned close, dared to put his lips to her ear, and of course Montague couldn't hear what he told her next. Shortly afterward, the gallant Richard fled in the opposite direction of where Montague had come.

He stood, uncertain, on the path while she delved her fingers into a clever pocket sewn into the folds of her skirting. Whatever it was she'd pulled from within was hidden from him, and he knew an unaccountable urge to see what it was she'd consigned to obscurity.

"Adriana." Determined not to startle her or have her once more flee, Montague crept forward onto the grass.

The alarmed squeak she uttered would have been amusing had their intertwined lives not been so tangled. "Pennington." She glanced over her shoulder as he drew closer, and her fingers were curled over whatever was in her palm. "What are you doing here?"

"Coming after you, obviously." Why else would he linger here in this terrible place? Every moment he stood there reminded him that across the park was the spot where his darling Penelope had breathed her last. "This isn't a safe place after dark. And I did warn you about going anywhere alone."

"Ah, yes, your immovable rules. Yet it's just now twilight." She transferred her attention to the Serpentine, whose color deepened and darkened the more the sun set. "I'd forgotten in the heat of the moment."

Deciding not to question her about the visitor, he came around into her line of sight. "There are specific reasons for the commands." That was all he would say, for he wasn't ready to lay bare his soul at this moment.

"Of course." She sighed. "How did you know I would be here?"

"Beyond asking your driver where you were?" The corners of his lips twitched with the beginnings of a smile. "Beyond that, you'd mentioned you enjoyed Hyde Park. I thought perhaps you might flee here under duress."

"Ah." A shiver racked her shoulders, for she'd gone off in a huff without thought to proper outerwear. "I'd forgotten that. Yet you remembered." A trace of awe lingered in her voice.

"Indeed. I *do* listen, even if you think the worst of me." The longer he lingered in her company, the more he couldn't forget the fires lit in his blood during that charged kiss, and damn him, he craved more of that connection, that sense of… belonging.

"Please leave, Pennington. I haven't the strength to argue with you at present."

He didn't particularly care for this defeated side to her. Where was the woman of spirit and lightning she'd been ever since they'd wed?

"I don't wish to argue." The surprise that skittered down his spine confirmed the notion. Perhaps it was time to introduce a new subject as well as a new way of interacting with her. "What have you there in your hand?"

"This?" Slowly, she uncurled her fingers to reveal a man's signet ring.

It was all too familiar, and his gut roiled as he recognized it. The small sapphire gleamed in the fading light, and he would wager the contents of his coffers that if he could examine it, there would be a griffin etched into one side of the shank with the Bassage coat of arms on the other.

Bloody hell.

"Where did you come by that?" he finally managed to inquire even as warning bells clanged in his mind.

"Happenstance, really." Adriana held up the signet ring. He forced a swallow into his suddenly tight throat.

"It used to be mine, once upon a time." Emotion graveled his voice. "I lost it at a gaming table years ago when I was but a novice gentleman new to the world of gambling." When she glanced up into his face, questions shadowed the dark depths of her eyes. "How is it in your possession?" He never forgave himself for the loss of that ring, for his father had died not long before he'd wagered it away.

The last connection to his father he'd had.

"My first husband was a bounder in every way a man could be." She turned the ring this way and that as she held it between her thumb and forefinger. "He was also a thief."

"I see."

"Apparently, one night on the street coming home from a tavern, he picked the pocket of a gentleman on Bond Street. After rendering the man unconscious, he stole everything of value from him. Dan brought home a haul of loot and dumped it on our kitchen table." She frowned as she looked at the bauble. "This ring was among the offerings."

"Did he gift it to you?"

"Ha!" Her chuckle held no mirth. "Dan never gave me anything except pain and heartbreak and embarrassment." Her hand trembled. "In any event, the ring appeared expensive and quite personal, and I certainly didn't want him to have it merely to pawn, so I took it one night when he was well into his cups."

"And then?" He desperately wanted to ask her about life with her bounder of a husband, ask about what he'd done to her that made her afraid of men and hate them—or perhaps hate him especially, but he kept his own counsel. There would be time later.

Perhaps.

The delicate tendons of her throat worked with a hard swallow. "I hid it in the hem of one of my gowns. Dan was truly a dull man and never knew it had gone missing from his stash of ill-gotten gain." She pressed her lips together. "I kept it over the years. Sometimes, I would pull it out merely to wonder over to whom it belonged, what sort of man he was, what his life must be like."

"Why?" A muscle in his cheek ticced. He couldn't find the words.

She shrugged. "It helped me escape my dismal life, escape from the reality of being beaten when Dan was in one of his violent moods." Another shiver racked her body. "In those times, I would imagine a life removed from struggle, far away from all I knew." In the last of the light, a blush stained her cheeks. "I created stories in my mind about the man to whom the ring belonged, convinced myself he would somehow find me, called to me by that ring." A tiny chuckle left her. "Then I would give him the bauble as a token of my affection, and that would usher in the beginning of a wonderful new… everything." She glanced at him. "Nothing but silly fantasy."

"I'm sorry. I had no idea, about any of it." And why should he? He'd not moved in the same circles as she, knew nothing about her other than the rumors, hadn't tried to make inroads into talking with her.

"It is a part of my history, what made me into the woman I am today." Adriana shrugged. She offered him the ring. "They were nothing more than the silly thoughts of an embittered woman to whom fate hadn't been kind."

His chest ached as if he'd been punched. Truly, he didn't know what to say. Despite his setbacks and his own trials, he'd been extraordinarily privileged. He'd not needed to worry about the basics of surviving. "Still, I am sorry all the same, for now you must endure marriage to me." A wave of desolation swept through him and left him chilled as he accepted her offering.

Was it given in the spirit of peace?

"As I said, fate isn't kind, and when that happens, there is no choice but to endure and hope for the best." She sounded so defeated that a wad of emotion lodged in his throat.

He much preferred her as the feisty storm. "Surely that will change. It must." Montague slipped the ring onto the pinky finger of his right hand. "Thank you for this," he said in a graveled whisper. It was the nicest gift anyone had given him in many years. She could have sold it. Had every right to do so in order to escape her husband and perhaps have a better life.

And oddly, he married the woman who'd saved it. A simple quirk of fate or merely a coincidence? Perhaps he could do something in the same vein for her.

She nodded. "I'm glad it's in the rightful hands of its owner."

"As am I." Common sense came rushing back. "You'll catch a chill." After he whipped off his greatcoat, he bundled it about her shoulders. "Quite bracing out here." A wave of protectiveness welled within him for her.

"Thank you." When she snuggled into the fabric and gratitude glinted in her eyes before she dropped her gaze, an ache began in his chest.

Finally, he saw his wife for the woman she was. Not for the inconvenience, not for a chore, not for an irritation. And neither for her flaws or the rumors surrounding her. She was merely a woman who'd been searching for peace and a sense of belonging for seemingly as long as he had.

Would it make a difference?

Again, he cleared his throat. He twisted the signet ring about his finger. The familiar weight of it put him back to that day when his father had given it to him. "You have no idea what this means." The emotion tried to choke him. "It was the only real connection I had to my father." Daring much, Montague pulled one side of the greatcoat more firmly around her. Shadows moved through her eyes. "Yes, I have his title and estates, but those are not personal. This was. He had this made for me on my 25th birthday, right before he perished. And now…" His voice broke, and he despised that show of weakness. "Now it's almost as if I can feel him close to me again."

Damn it all. Why had he shared so much about himself?

For long moments, she watched him in wariness. Finally, she nodded. "I'm glad. Perhaps this might help you to heal. I… I suspect you are sorely in need of that but haven't a clue of how to make that happen."

For the first time since he'd met and married her, a certain bond had formed between them. It was as if he'd been given a hint to the answers he'd desperately been seeking over the years. "Perhaps we both need that."

Give and take. She'd made the opening salvo which required him to respond in kind, but that would mean letting her close to a certain extent.

Did he have the mental fortitude necessary to survive this union?

CHAPTER EIGHT

ADRIANA WAS OUT to sea on a variety of emotions. Never would she have thought that running away from this man would have brought them a bit closer through sharing bits from their past, yet here they were, both struggling to bring those emotions under control or even hide them. The fact he'd opened up to her, hadn't met her in anger, stole some of her own ire.

She took in a deep breath and let it ease slowly out. "I hope you won't offer that ring at a gaming table again." What else was there to say? Sadness pinged deep inside her chest, for she'd kept that ring safe for so many years that it had become a talisman of sorts. Now that she'd given it up, she couldn't help but think some of her hopes had slipped away, unnoticed. When another shiver racked her shoulders, she burrowed into her husband's greatcoat and allowed a moment to luxuriate in the intoxicating scent of him.

"I am well beyond the novice stage." Had his voice always been such a pleasant baritone? "But I can assure you this signet ring will never leave my possession again."

"That is all to the good." Slowly, Adriana rose to her feet. Now that the sun was nearly set, the temperature in the air had cooled significantly. *Oh, I hope winter doesn't come too early.* But it only made her wish to walk through the park and breathe in the smells of wood fires.

"Uh, Adriana?" There was a tentativeness in the inquiry she hadn't heard before.

"Yes?"

"Who was that man you were talking with earlier before I arrived?"

Dear heavens. He'd witnessed that meeting? She looked at him through the gathering shadows of twilight, but remarkably, there was no anger in his visage. Had this night somehow become enchanted? She pulled the greatcoat tighter about her person. "That was Mr. Richard Somerford. He's a younger son of a viscount, and someone I call a friend. One of the only ones who stuck by me after the scandalbroth following my husband's death."

"Is he—was he—a suitor?"

Heat suffused her cheeks. "Not to me. I never took him seriously, but he remains fiercely loyal." When Pennington didn't look away from her face, she sighed. "He thinks to protect me. Tried to get me to safety when things were at their roughest with my husband. I warned him off to keep Dan from doing something horrible to him."

"And now he wishes to lure you from me because he believes me to be of the same ilk." It wasn't a question.

"Yes." There was no point in denying it, for if the earl had overheard the conversation, that would only cause more friction between them.

In the shadows, a trace of vulnerability showed in his eyes, gone with his next blink. "Is that what you want? To be free of me, my temper, my reputation?" His swallow was audible. "My boorish treatment of you thus far?" The last was said in such a low pitch, she was obliged to step closer to him in order to hear it.

Was he giving her a way out, to walk away without drama or

more vitriol between them? An ache set up around her heart at the unexpected kindness as well as that crack in his outer shell. "No, it's not what I want. As I've said, I've rebuffed him multiple times." She shrugged and was grateful for the weight of his greatcoat about her shoulders. "I am married to you, Montague. No matter what happens, you have my fidelity and discretion."

Would he take the gift in the spirit that it was offered? And more to the point, would he give her the same latitude?

"Even after everything?"

"You may be a beast and I a murderess, but that doesn't mean we cannot have honor between us." The longer she stared at him, the more trembles played up and down her spine. She had the acute sensation she was standing, wavering, waiting at the edge of a steep precipice. Would he push her down or would he offer a helping hand? And if he faltered too, would he accept her assistance?

"I… I don't… It has been such a long time since anyone has shown me…" It was maddening how he couldn't finish the sentence, for she desperately wished to know what he would have said.

But perhaps the moment had passed. "All right then." She tamped down the rising tide of disappointment. "I will leave you to your plans for the night. No doubt you have a woman to take to your bed."

Why did I say that? Especially when they had made strides to bridge the gulf between them. Yet it had been uppermost in her mind since the nuptial ceremony. Did he have a mistress? Would she be shown the same consideration she'd given him?

Annoyance flashed across his face. "I do, actually."

Of course he did.

Cold desolation swept in to obliterate the tentative understanding she'd extended. "Is it beyond you to declare peace? Do you despise marriage that much, or it is merely me you take great joy in antagonizing?" To her mortification, tears stung the backs of her eyelids. Perhaps she didn't realize just how much she'd wanted acceptance, perhaps friendship, from this man who was her husband.

"None of those things is true." As she stood, muscles taut and ready to run, a slow, wicked grin curved his lips, and the gesture completely transformed his face. Already sinfully handsome, he was now strikingly so, and with the breeze ruffling through his hair that wanted to curl, he was nothing short of delicious. "Let me show you why I said what I did."

Before she could form a protest or even a response, he swiftly closed the distance between them. One second, she stood stewing in outrage and the next she was caught neatly into his embrace and his lips were pressed to hers.

While her heart beat out a rapid tattoo, Adriana couldn't help but rest her palms upon his chest. She pulled away to peer up into his face. "I thought you—" Oh, dear heavens, he gave her that grin again, and this time flutters moved through her lower belly.

"I wished to see if that connection, that reaction, that energy from our last kiss was merely a fluke."

In a way, that made sense, for it had been *quite* a kiss. "Was it?" She could scarcely force out the words from her suddenly tight throat.

"It was not." One of his dark eyebrows arched. "Shall I continue, or would you like to berate me further?"

"Please, continue, but you haven't answered my question of—"

He quelled her words with another kiss, and this one bordered on primal and was reminiscent of the one that had them crashing together earlier that afternoon. With one hand, he cradled the back of her head and the other he slipped to the curve of her arse and brought her close, so incredibly close, to his body. With a soft sound of acceptance, Adriana clutched at his shoulders and returned his kisses as best she could.

Oh, he was glorious! The sensations zipping through her were wonderous!

She marveled that two men could be so incredibly different when it came to showing desire and taking the same from a partner. Where her first husband had only perfunctorily kissed her, and only when she'd asked him to, the kisses she'd shared with Montague had the power to thoroughly transform her as a woman.

I'm drowning.

Perhaps she was naught but a desperate woman, or perhaps she just needed the fulfillment of the primal promise he offered, but she clung to him and kissed him—almost devoured him—without shame. In him, in each meeting of his mouth, in every touch of his tongue to hers. This had been one of the components that had been missing in her last marriage, this feeling as if Pennington needed her to complete a specific part of him, and that he was vital to her composition as well.

The earl wrenched away. "Hold!" He caught at the greatcoat as it slipped from one of her shoulders. "It's hardly proper to keep on in this vein when anyone could come upon us. The park isn't safe at night."

Adriana's head swam with the abrupt change in topic. What on earth had occurred here that had made him so wary? "It was lovely while it lasted."

"Have you been thoroughly pleasured at any time during your life?" he asked in a low voice that brimmed with mystery.

"No, but—"

"Then we are not finished." With a hand to the small of her back, Pennington ushered her back up the path toward the entrance gate where his familiar closed carriage waited.

Anticipation tingled down her spine while he handed her into the vehicle. Still stunned and drifting in a cloud of warmth leftover from those heated kisses, she collapsed rather than sat on one of the well-squabbed benches. Baffled by his change of attitude, she frowned as he talked with Charles the driver.

"Please, take a tour about Hyde Park at your leisure before heading back to St. James Place. Lady Pennington and I are in no hurry."

"As you like, Your Lordship."

Then the earl joined her in the carriage and firmly closed the door behind him. As an added surprise, he sat next to her on the bench, and immediately, his presence, his scent, the heat of him overwhelmed her.

"Shall we take up where we left off?"

The rumble of his voice tickled through her chest, and just like every other time, before she could even form an answer, he'd interrupted her thought processes. Grasping her about the waist, he unceremoniously hauled her into his lap so that she straddled his lap, her knees on the bench. A squeak of surprise left her throat. Her heartbeat raced as if she'd run here from France. "What are you about?"

Truly, was she that big of a ninny she couldn't suspect?

"Setting out to seduce my wife."

When he would have claimed her lips again, she quickly pressed the fingers of one hand to his mouth. Despite the waves of awareness shivering over her, there was a specific answer she needed before they could proceed. "Do you have a mistress, Pennington? This goes no farther if so."

"I admire your determination and search for the truth." The words were jumbled, but he took her hand and pressed his lips to the back of her wrist. His greatcoat fell from her shoulders to pool on the floor of the carriage. "However, no. I haven't taken a mistress—or anyone else—into my bed for the last two months."

"Why?" Tremors of need made themselves known in her lower belly and throbbed between her thighs.

He shrugged. "Not in the right frame of mind? Wished to be alone with my thoughts? Let grief and memories take too much of a foothold during that time?" When the earl sucked her index finger into his mouth and swirled his tongue around the digit, she shivered.

Dear heavens. Had he always been this potent?

"Yet you wish to initiate relations now, with me, even after I told you I would never give you access to my body?" Gently, she took back her hand.

That dratted eyebrow quirked upward again. "Is that still your stance?" Slowly, he drew a hand up her leg and beneath her skirting to rest on her outer thigh. "You certainly seem to enjoy kissing me."

Heat swept through her cheeks. "I… I…" Yesterday, she'd been furious with him, livid perhaps, but after their exchange in his dressing room followed by the conversation in the park where he'd revealed a different side of himself, now she was more confused than ever. One thing was perfectly clear. She wanted this man—her husband—and if it was merely for the chance at physical release, that niggling something she'd never had from her first husband, then she would analyze that later. "Is not a woman allowed to change her mind?"

What sort of woman did it make her that she couldn't wait to bed him so soon after marrying him under duress?

Pathetic, that's what.

For the first time since she'd met him, he chuckled and the addictive sound swept away her thoughts of the moment, but he didn't answer her with words. Instead, he claimed her mouth in a kiss no less passionate than before.

"After all, there is no scandal in it," she whispered against his lips, still attempting to make sense of this new decision that went against everything she'd formerly believed.

"Imagine us doing something the gossips cannot touch for once." Then he set out to kiss her senseless all over again. When finished, he added, "No, there's not."

"The driver will hear."

He snorted. "It's nothing he hasn't heard before."

That took a bit of the heat out of her. "Ah. Your string of conquests." When she made to move from his lap, he huffed.

"You knew my history. I may be the biggest rake and the worst man in London, but I'm here now. With you, and for the moment, my tastes and intents have shifted."

The words held the ring of truth, and that was more than she'd had yesterday. For long moments she peered into his eyes. Adriana didn't care if she was perhaps desperate; she'd been forced to be strong for more years than she could count. Now, though, she was in a marriage she hadn't wished for with a man she didn't know if she could trust or even live with, she would take what she wanted, as everyone else in her life had done from her.

And she wanted him, wanted to feel his hands on her body, wanted to join with him for nothing more than mutual desire without worrying over what would come next. She gave him back as good as he gave her, and all the while she tugged on his cravat until the knot unraveled and she could press her lips to the skin of his neck she exposed.

To the earl's credit, he was more than willing to let her explore, for he did the same to her. His hands were everywhere, gliding over her skin, caressing places she'd not been touched before, awakening parts of her she had no idea had been neglected. No wonder he was a favorite with the demimonde; he certainly knew how to arouse and tease with tongue, fingers, and teeth. While he continued to caress her leg, he drew his lips down the column of her throat to nip at the swells of her breasts. She watched him through hooded eyes, but the dark gloom inside the vehicle prevented her from clearly reading his emotions.

Seconds later, he had the line of small buttons at the back of her gown undone, and as the garment gaped, he eased both layers of fabric down until her breasts were exposed for his perusal. Words flew through Adriana's mind, that she wasn't his usual style, that he wouldn't want her because she possessed too many curves, was too fleshy, that she was too old, but the second he closed his lips onto the tight bud of a nipple, she forgot everything in order to simply concentrate on the wave of erotic pleasure slamming into her.

"Oh!" She shot upward on her knees, but that action merely put her breast more firmly in his hold.

Pennington hummed his approval and continued the cycle of licking, suckling, soothing with the flat of his tongue. Then he switched attention to the other breast and began all over again. He used the opportunity to squeeze her arse cheek, glide his fingers over the flesh between her thighs, gently exploring, teasing her into a state of constant strain.

"You are shaking," he whispered and continued his ministrations.

"This is all so different." She bit back a scream when he sucked hard at her nipple. "I didn't realize—"

"—that you could still be very much a virgin despite the fact you'd been bedded before?" Once more, he claimed her lips and at the same time he strummed his fingers over the swelling button at the center of her, the place where no one had ever paid attention to, except for her own fingers at times.

"Awk!" Adriana's back arched, her body shook; apparently, she had no more control over her being, not while the earl manipulated her as if she were a marionette puppet and he her master. "Oh! Montague, yes, please, do that *again!*"

A blatant guffaw issued from their driver, but she didn't care. There was plenty of time for embarrassment later, but not while the earl teased her nubbin with varying degrees of friction. Already having been primed, both from his kisses and sharing tonight as well as their arguments and heated words from the moment they'd met, it took very little effort for her to fall over the edge into surprising bliss.

A choked cry was yanked from her throat as she flew through the heavens. Rapid, strong throbbing loosed deep in her core, and she gasped from it. So much better than she'd managed to achieve with her own fingers, and never had she been treated to such from her first husband.

"Mercy," she mumbled while she slumped against his chest, her arms loosely about his shoulders. Her body shook with residual tremors. "That was quite something."

"The first course, my dear." Then he moved his hand between them once more, but this time he fumbled with the buttons on his front falls.

Oh, what she wouldn't give to see his hot length, but when the wide head of his shaft glided along her slick flesh, her mind skittered sideways again. This was truly going to happen! Their wedding night delayed by a day, and never would she have imagined it taking place in a carriage, but here they were. She lifted her head, found his gaze in the darkness of the carriage. He gave nothing away as to his thoughts or feelings, but she didn't mind. Not in this moment. Right now, nothing existed in the world except joining with this man and taking the pleasure she'd been so long denied.

He dug his fingers into her hips, maneuvered her to where he wanted, and then he flashed a grin, his teeth white in the dim illumination from a gas light as they turned out of Hyde Park. "Slam down upon me while I thrust upward," he instructed in a tense whisper. No doubt his hold on control was severely taxed.

She'd bared nodded when he shifted, moved his hips, and then speared into her, penetrating her body and tugged her down over his shaft until she was fully and irrevocably impaled upon him. "Oh!" Indescribable sensations slammed into her, and for one second, she paused merely to revel in them.

With a grunt, the earl widened his stance then nipped at the underside of her jaw. "Quickly." The growled command sent heightened awareness over her skin.

It was awkward at first, this joining with him while in such a foreign position and an engaged carriage to boot, but with his guidance and her need to chase a second release, Adriana managed it. Soon enough they moved in tandem, and it was nothing like she'd ever experienced before. Frenzied need met white-hot desire and left them in a tangle of limbs as he stroked in and out.

Without shame, she gyrated her hips, took him in as deep as she could, and with every thrust that he made, pressure coiled tight deep within her belly. It grew and grew until she couldn't stand it any longer, but still she wanted—needed—more. It had been so long since she'd felt vital or even worthy, she wished this coupling would never end.

But her breathing quickened as she was thrown closer to that edge. Pennington's thrusts grew more erratic. Their pants blended together; their moans marked the time. The scrape of his jacket against her sensitive nipples lent another level of pleasure to their play.

Then, before she was ready, that coiling pressure broke, and Adriana shattered in his hold. Perhaps it was her sharp intake of breath, or perhaps all women were the same when they broke, but he kissed her with a savageness that matched what they were doing, took the sound of her scream of repletion into himself. She fell down, down, down even as she went flying into a void stripped of all light and sound.

He thrust again and again, ground his hips into hers before he, too, followed her into that vortex where the greatest bliss was the currency of the land. A soft curse echoed in her ear. Warmth jetted deep into her core, and she slumped into his chest, her limbs as weak and limp as if she were a newborn lamb.

Eventually, Adriana came back to her senses and stirred, but he didn't release her from the loose embrace he held her in. "Well, we can safely say that the tension building between us has finally broken," she joked in a breathless whisper.

"Indeed, it has." But he didn't flash that grin again, and it was almost as if he were retreating back into himself. Was he afraid or ashamed or even angry? It was impossible to tell. Instead, he turned his face to the window. "Please do not think this means I suddenly have fallen in love with you. I don't even know if I like you outside of this moment. It merely means we were both overcome with desire and emotion which required an outlet."

How could she be angry with him when it was the truth? "Then it's a good thing I'm clever enough to know intercourse doesn't equate to romance." And unless they rubbed along beyond the physical, this couldn't happen again. "I thought I was in love before and that ended horribly. I'm not keen to do that again."

He didn't need to know that was a partial lie, for she had never been successful in banishing that tiny little dream.

"My heart is my own, Adriana. It must be that way, *stay* that way, for I am not strong enough to survive the breaking of such again." Montague moved her from his lap and deposited her on the bench beside him without ceremony. "I am sorry, but in this, I suppose I am destined to be what I have always been, since…"

"…you met with disappointment and disillusionment, and it kept you company," she finished softly for him. "I understand." Perhaps in that and in shared grief, she could finally bond with him, help him to heal and he might do the same for her.

The key was to meet each day as it came and try not to let him push her into anger so he could hide in his.

Heaven help me.

CHAPTER NINE

October 18, 1817

I T HAD BEEN two days since the tension, need, and longing Adriana had carried inside for years had suddenly broken, all due to her husband.

When they'd come together in the carriage that night, she'd had no idea what to expect, but even in that he was powerful and all-consuming, and she'd been thoroughly claimed by him. They had a bond now based on pure carnality certainly, but it was there, and she hoped they could grow from that.

Yet, how would any of that work if they both remained mired in what had hurt them in the past? Truthfully, she'd only seen Montague for dinner the past two nights, for he'd had business with Parliament as well as other duties for his title and charities, and she'd retreated to her rooms in order to make sense of how that bout of frantic intercourse might change their relationship.

If at all. Everything was still too new, too overwhelming, but with a few select members of the staff, she was finding her footing in her capacity as a countess, and what she wanted above all things was to create a refuge or a salon that would assist women who'd been abused or neglected within their marriages. Yet how to help others overcome that stigma when she couldn't bear to talk about it herself?

To her credit, she'd been busy as well. There had been long sessions with the modiste and her seamstresses, meetings with the housekeeper and cook. She'd also made inroads into meeting the remainder of the staff at Bassage House, to say nothing of taking the time to answer correspondence and accept a handful of invitations that had been proffered to her as the Countess of Pennington. And though it had gone against her husband's dictates, she'd visited Hyde Park after a stint of shopping on Bond Street.

By herself. It hadn't been that she'd deliberately set out to antagonize him, she simply hadn't thought about asking anyone to come with her, for she'd lived a solitary life for years despite having people around her.

People who hadn't cared.

As she accepted a cup of tea from Pearson and nodded her thanks when a footman brought her a plate filled with her favorite breakfast offerings, the earl joined her in the morning room and took a seat beside her at the round table. Her jaw dropped in surprise. The bit of sausage she'd offered to Satan beneath the table tumbled from her fingers. The cat pounced upon it with a tiny growl of possession.

"What are you doing here? I rather thought you would remain abed until at least noon." At times, he spent time at his club, but last night he was home but cloistered in his rooms doing what only God knew, for he hadn't sought her out. Had he gotten wind of her excursion yesterday when she hadn't taken a groom or a maid? Would he lecture or bluster?

"I was hungry." As if that explained the aberrant behavior. While Pearson brought him a cup of black coffee, the earl glanced at her. "Unless you would rather not linger in my company?" A tiny glimmer of vulnerability showed in his stormy eyes, but it was gone with his next blink.

"Uh…" She glanced at the butler, who gave her a barely noticeable shrug. "That would be lovely. Thank you. Er, I mean lovely if you stay to breakfast."

What did his presence here mean, though?

He grunted in response and then tucked into his own breakfast plate as if he'd not eaten in days while she watched him with speculation. It was a pity the day had started with rain, for he would have been mouth-watering in the sunlight. As it was, she had trouble concentrating on her own food with him so near. The scent of him teased her nose but the heat of him, his undeniable presence called to her, invited her touch, especially now that he wore a jacket of sapphire superfine that hugged his shoulders and chest like a lover's caress, but she quelled the urge. Until she knew how they would interact together following that night in the carriage or even what he wanted from her this morning, she would keep her own counsel.

That didn't stop her from wanting to feel his body against hers again, to know he was a skilled enough lover that he would see to her pleasure first before seeking her own as he'd done in the carriage. Those were heady thoughts indeed, and she would be drunk of them if she'd let herself.

By the time he'd finished his first cup of coffee, the earl seemed more relaxed than he'd been when he'd arrived. A huff escaped him, and he nodded to himself as if coming to a decision he'd debated with for quite some time.

"Adriana?"

"Yes?" She glanced at him from over the rim of her teacup. Would he lay down another set of rules?

"I would like to offer you the use of my library, should you wish it."

"What?" As shock plowed into her being, the grip on her teacup went lax. A few drops of amber liquid dripped to stain the lace of the tablecloth, but Pearson was quickly at her side to dab at the mess with a slightly dampened napkin. Perhaps she'd heard her husband wrong. "I beg your pardon? I thought that was your sanctuary." It wasn't a question.

"It still is, but that doesn't mean we cannot share the space." A slight flush rose over his cravat. "I have thought the matter over, and I wish to have you make use of the library whenever it might please you." He shrugged, stared at Satan as the cat jumped up onto the table and set out to investigate the contents of her plate. "I rather suspect you have been without books, and you miss them."

"How could you possibly know that?" she managed to whisper through a tight throat as she set the teacup into its saucer. "My first husband had disliked me to read or use books for any reason. He hadn't liked I was more intelligent than he." When she looked at the butler, his shock no doubt mirrored her own.

"An enthusiast of literature always knows when there is a kindred spirit about." The words, accompanied by a tiny, tentative grin had the power to steal her breath. He took hold of the cat and then set the errant feline back onto the floor, but not before Satan stole a kipper with an extended claw.

"I *have* missed books." She poked at the food on her plate with her fork. "When I returned to my parents' house, I'd used the lending library since I couldn't afford to buy my own copies." The sheer enormity of the gift he'd given her boggled her mind. "Thank you," she said in a near-whisper.

"You are welcome, and now you have shelves of books at your disposal." A muscle ticced in his cheek. "If you accept."

"Truly?"

"Yes." He offered another grin, this one more confident, and she nearly fell off her chair. It completely transformed his face from a brooding, angry recluse to an approachable, interesting man with secrets in his eyes. "It is the least I can do."

"Then of course I accept. Quite frankly, I cannot wait to explore." She met his gaze, almost tumbled into the stormy depths of his eyes. "Uh, explore the room," she quickly added lest he think she was demented with wanting him.

"Good." He returned to eating his breakfast, shoveling in golden mounds of scrambled eggs as if they would soon vanish from existence.

The cat, now carrying his prize in his mouth, darted from the room.

Adriana took a few bites of her own meal, but her appetite had fled in the face of anticipation. "Do you enjoy reading, Montague?" How much did she enjoy saying his name? It felt so powerful, so naughty, so freeing at the same time.

"I do. Along with painting, it is how I attempt to bring order and peace to my life." He regarded her with curiosity. "Sometimes, I lose myself for hours within the pages of my favorites. What I have found over the years is that there is always something to be learned." His tiny shrug moved his shoulders and allowed the jacket to pull tight across that tempting breadth.

"Do you have a favorite?" Imagine being able to talk about books with one's husband. She reeled from the differences in her marriages.

"Recently, I have become fascinated with the work of Mary Wollstonecraft. In her book, *A Vindication of the Rights of Woman*, she has strong stances about the ills of society. I particularly enjoy where she argues that women are not naturally inferior to men, but appear to be only because they lack education. I have always maintained women should have the same access to knowledge that men take for granted."

"That is a lovely concept," she said in some shock.

"Yes." Excitement rang in his voice. "She suggests that both men and women should be treated as rational beings and imagines a social order founded on reason. Even dares to put forth the notion that men and women are equal."

"I heard her speak once, sneaked away from my house while my husband was in his cups. It was quite enlightening as well as inspiring." Adriana narrowed her eyes on him. "Do you believe what she says has merit?"

"Oh, indeed. I carry her notions forth while I'm doing my duty in Parliament. The current laws need to be changed, for without that, London will lose all the prestige it once had." He offered her a genuine smile, and it sent little flutters through her lower belly. "I, and a handful of others, fight for equality of all people in England, but we are up against staunch views and outdated notions. It is disheartening at times, for I fear progress will fall to tradition."

"Keep fighting, Montague." She appreciated his progressive viewpoints. "I am only just realizing how far my reach suddenly is as your countess, and how I can also affect change with that." Later she would tell him of her ideas for a charity. "I don't take that lightly."

"At least I am able to vent my spleen on the floor of the House of Lords. It helps with the internal struggle."

"I can only imagine." Oh, he would look fierce and lovely locked in arguments with aging lords set in their ways! But perhaps they should return to the subject at hand before she did something stupid. "For years, I have adored art in all its forms, especially paintings. A few of the masters are my favorites. I could sit and study their work for hours." Though it felt as if she were babbling, she didn't care. He had extended an olive branch, and she wouldn't waste it. "But for more modern art, I have come to appreciate the portraits and landscapes of Monsieur René Depardieu. His brushstrokes compel me to look closer; his work pulls me in until I can almost imagine I am in those paintings. As if he has left a hidden piece of his soul somewhere in those pictures."

"I see." Another flush rose above his cravat. Was he embarrassed for her or the situation? "He does seem to have a grasp on light and movement."

"Yes, and brushstrokes, and the use of subtle colors and shading." Her mind jogged to the portraits she'd seen in the earl's dressing room. How had he come to painting, and had he done anything recently? And probably more pressing of all, who were those women with the slashes of red across the canvas?

She had a chance to ask about his past since he was relaxed and in a decent mood, but not here. Not with the butler and a footman hovering. Slowly, Adriana rose to her feet. "Come to the library with me. Show me your favorite books and I shall discover if you have mine."

Surprise lined his face. Even Pearson paused in his puttering to stare. "You wish to spend time with me outside of mundane functions?" There was no mistaking the shock in Pennington's voice.

"Yes." She nodded lest he misunderstand. "Why not?"

"I… I have kept people away for so long that no one has wanted to be around me." His jaw worked but no further words escaped. "Well, no one except Ashbury."

Though the muscles in her stomach grew taut, Adriana forged ahead. "Perhaps it is time to see how you like bringing a bit of light into your life."

The butler animated himself first. "Uh, Your Lordship, you *do* have a late luncheon on your schedule with Lord and Lady Aldren. They both wish to meet your new countess."

A twinge of disappointment went through her chest. "Never mind. This can keep."

For the space of a few heartbeats, Pennington rested his gaze on her. Then he shook his head. "Send my regrets, Pearson. Talking with my wife is more important just now."

Once more, both Adriana and the butler reeled with shock.

Pearson spoke first. "I shall see that a fire is lit in the library, Your Lordship should you wish to spend the afternoon there. It will take off the chill from the air."

"Thank you, Pearson." Montague continued to look at her as if he couldn't quite figure her out. Once the butler and footman left the room, he nodded. "If you find the library amenable, perhaps you will tell me about your first husband? I cannot imagine someone who doesn't like books. It is a foreign concept to me."

A hesitant smile of her own spread across her face. "I would like that." This man was a puzzle to solve. Did she have the patience and fortitude to do so? Could she trust that he wouldn't turn into the beast again?

It all remained to be seen.

Some thirty minutes later, after Montague had shown her the most prominent features of the room—handsome, dark furniture that fairly exclaimed the space a man's abode, buttery-soft dark leather on the chairs and sofas, deep maroon curtains and rugs, a wheeled ladder that allowed a person to reach the set of double shelves that ran the length of two sides of the room—Adriana had sank into one of the sofas with her legs tucked beneath her and a modest stack of books reposing on the floor beside her.

The books within the library spanned every conceivable subject she could ever want or dream of. He had several shelves of fiction, including the popular novels and gothic works proper ladies were never supposed to read. Though she'd removed a few of them from the shelves as he followed her through the room, she'd also taken possession of other volumes like a collection of sonnets from Shake-speare, poetry from Keats, and a rather well-loved copy of Homer's *Odyssey*.

With a sigh of contentment, Adriana reached for the first book on her stack, but a comment from her husband gave her pause.

"Tell me about Mr. Roberts." He'd come to rest at the fireplace with its cheerful flames dancing behind an ornate metal grate and rested a hand on the high mantel.

She frowned. "I would much rather talk about literature or even you." And now that she had a pile of books to dive into, the thought of telling him of that shameful time in her life no longer appealed.

Shadows flitted across his face. "Not today. I don't wish to destroy our forward momentum, and you *did* promise."

"Fair enough." Perhaps if she gave him something, he might do the same in return, and that might foster trust between them. With a last lingering glance at her book pile, she flicked her gaze to his face. "How much do you know about me?"

"Surprisingly little outside of rumor and gossip."

A wave of bitterness fell over her. "We are all judged on that it seems." A sense of restlessness invaded, so she left the relative safety of the sofa and padded to a window, stared out at the rain and shiny, wet streets. "All my life, I wanted to make my parents proud, but when I didn't take in my first or second Seasons seemingly ages ago, there was more disappointment there than anything else." She lifted a hand and traced a raindrop with a fingertip. "Then, as I matured, my body betrayed me by insisting on developing voluptuous curves that render me plump instead of the thinness current fashion demands."

"That is hardly something to despair." Amusement threaded through his baritone. "Extra flesh is quite enticing in certain situations, and your modiste has certainly done wonders with enhancing your figure thus far."

"Thank you. She'd delivered a few day dresses already." Heat jumped into her cheeks at the thought of him noticing her form and the frocks. "I suppose some men like that look." The earl had certainly enjoyed her breasts and hips in the carriage… With a shake of her head, she resumed her narrative. "Regardless, Raphaelite women haven't been chased by marriage-minded gentlemen for years—mistresses yes, but that is a different animal—so I was often overlooked in favor of other forms of beauty."

"I don't know how. You are quite strident and determined."

"They are leadership qualities." Adriana snorted and shot a glance to his face. He wasn't openly laughing at her, but amusement danced in his eyes and a budding grin had curved his lips. "Perhaps you bring out the worst in me."

"Perhaps, but I am adamant those traits aren't necessarily horrid things," he answered in a soft voice. "Not many women have stood toe to toe with me and shouted me down, let alone slammed a door in my face. Or slapped me. Or dumped my arse onto a bedchamber floor." The admiration in his expression sent confusion into her mind.

"Ah." Was he trying to… flirt? How odd and somewhat pleasant. But why? She didn't know, refused to ask lest it break the spell. "Eventually, my chances of making a match slipped away, and my family grew more concerned with raising Sybil, for even early on it was obvious she was the true beauty of the Stapleton family."

"Beauty comes in many different forms, Adriana. Remember that," he cautioned in that same soft voice. "Whatever happened in your past to bring you down or cause you to doubt yourself should be tossed to the rubbish heap."

"It's a difficult proposition when one has been inundated by it, taught again and again that one is indeed not worthy." Though she hated the catch in her voice, she couldn't help it. This was her life's story. Yes, there was shame there, but there was also the opportunity to rise above it. Perhaps now was that time. "When I met a struggling merchant at a rout, I was completely taken by his cordial manner and his decent looks. That's how desperate I was to escape… everything." She frowned at her reflection in the window glass. "Though he and I had shared one dance and a handful of polite words, my parents jumped on that opening."

"Ah, I see." The earl hadn't moved from his position at the fireplace. "Before you knew it, you were engaged to that man who'd no doubt shown the polite world a façade, and then you were even more quickly married."

"Yes." The muscles in her stomach clenched. Tears climbed her throat, for now she would have to confess all to him. "Soon after that, the bottom fell out, and my life tilted sideways."

CHAPTER TEN

M ONTAGUE WATCHED AS his wife's expression changed into a mask of fear and hopelessness when she turned to face him, but he didn't leave his post at the fireplace for fear she would retreat into herself and not finish her story. After she'd been uncommonly happy upon availing herself of his library shelves, she had become a haunted shell of herself, but he needed to know her history in her own words.

To understand her.

To better get along with her.

To help her work through that pain, and in return, perhaps she might do the same for him.

When he was ready.

By sharing the library with her, he had made great strides into accepting her into his life as his wife. Yes, there were still obstacles and gulfs in their path, yet this was a start.

"Did Mr. Roberts reveal his true self immediately after you wed?"

"Of course not. Men who are abusers never do." She rubbed her hands up and down her arms. Was she cold or needing comfort? To her credit, though, Adriana kept her gaze on him. "I was married to that louse for eight years." Shadows clouded her eyes. "Eight long years," she repeated in a lower voice.

"Were you ever happy in that union?" When Satan sauntered into the room as if he owned the place and then wound about Montague's boots, he tamped down the urge to smile lest she think he made jest of her.

"I suppose there were chunks of time where I might have been close." The tendons in her throat worked with a hard swallow, but she didn't turn back to the window in an effort to hide. "During the first few years, Dan and I got on well enough. He was polite and affable as a new husband should be. We fought on a regular basis."

Despite the sober subject matter, Montague snorted. "I cannot imagine that sort of behavior from you."

Her lips twitched with the beginnings of a smile, but it never fully materialized. "None of your cheek now, Pennington."

How was it possible he vastly preferred it when she referred to him by his Christian name?

Before he could analyze that, Adriana continued with her story. "Those first few years I could have been happy, but then Dan's luck changed. His shipping business encountered a few hiccups. Textiles went missing. A few storms took out two of his vessels. Vendors left in favor of partnering with other, more truthful outfits."

"I suppose I could guess at the rest of your story if you don't wish to share all." He pushed off the mantel but couldn't quite bring himself to go to her side.

"You deserve the whole sordid tale, and perhaps in the telling of it, I will grasp at some peace, for I have carried its weight for far too long by myself."

He frowned. "Your family doesn't know the truth?"

"No." The word sounded pulled from a tight throat. "There was already enough scandal trailing after me that I didn't wish to add to it, and besides, Sybil would have her first Season soon after the ordeal

ended. Everything the Stapletons did and had went toward that."
When she shrugged, she looked much like a lost waif. "Sybil was our
last hope for a decent marriage and connections. By that time, Papa
had discovered the gaming tables."

"Ah." They had lived very different lives, and now more than ever
he wished to make up for that fact.

To protect her.

"For a while, I kept busy ordering the rooms we rented in a board-
ing house at the edge of Mayfair. I had silly dreams in my head that
Dan and I would soon bond and grow close, or that I would become
pregnant, that we could become a family. At least then, I would at
least have purpose and make someone proud." Her voice broke on the
last word, and Montague's chest tightened. "Yet, none of those things
happened. As the business continued to fail and coin became tight—
my husband had already gone through the dowry Papa gave him—
Dan turned to drinking as his vice of choice." A hard note had entered
her normally dulcet tones. "And when that didn't relieve his worry, he
started beating me."

"Dear God." As shock slammed into him, Montague stared at her.
Right before his eyes, she seemed to retreat into herself, into her
memories, shrinking, hugging her arms about herself no doubt in an
effort to appear as small as she could.

To hide.

No longer did she see him, apparently. "At first, when they happened, he promptly apologized, vowed to never do it again." Shadows
scudded across her face. "But the more he drank, the greater his
business losses, the more he would hit me. Always in places that were
easily concealed by clothing, lest our landlady see, or my family
suspect, when we took Sunday dinner with them."

Bile climbed his throat. He curled one of his hands into fists, for he
would have defended this woman against such a bounder. "There is no
excuse for such behavior," he managed to choke out.

"I agree, but Dan considered it his right as my husband, because I belonged to him." This time, she turned back to the window, but the gloom outside was enough that Montague could read her reflection in the glass.

"Bloody hell."

"Eventually, he didn't care if the bruises were noticeable. His temper was always greater in the middle of the night when he came home from the taverns." She shook her head. "On those nights, he would beat me, tell me it was my fault that his fortunes had diminished, that I wasn't supporting him as a wife should."

"Adriana, I—"

She continued despite his interruption. "He would force himself on me night after night, even after I bid him nay. For years." When she looked over her shoulder at him and that pain was mired deep in her eyes, Montague wanted to retch. "Why would I wish to bond with him when he was nothing but horrid?"

The magnitude of what she'd survived slammed into him, made him reel with shock and horror. "How long did that go on?"

"Three years, perhaps?" Her voice was devoid of all inflection as she stared out the window, but her face in profile looked ready to crumple. "There were times when I wanted the pain, the fear to end, and I considered throwing myself into the Thames, letting the water close over me and gain a blessed surcease to what my life had become."

Good God. She'd considered suicide. "How did you pull yourself out of it?" The strength she possessed staggered him. Where she'd had no choice but to meet her demons day after day, he'd hid from his.

"I became with child. That gave me new hope." Her admission, in a soft voice had him once more searching out her gaze.

"But, you haven't talked of a child… Do you parents care for it?"

"No." So much pain and emotion lay infused in that one word, it poked at his own. "I lost the pregnancy at nearly three months, perhaps due to continued beatings and the anxiety they caused. After that, I didn't conceive again."

"I'm so sorry for your loss." He well knew what a loss of that magnitude felt like, how one didn't easily heal from that, and it put them on the same footing. "How did you manage to continue living after that?"

Please tell me how.

"I don't know that I did." Adriana turned to face him once more. Her eyes were haunted, her face wreathed in sorrow. "There is not a day that goes by I don't think about that child, wonder about what it would have looked like, how it would have acted, what sort of personality it would have had." Tears welled in her eyes. When one escaped to her cheek, he felt that drop deep in his soul as if he'd been punched. "After that, my marriage deteriorated further. Those last two years were hell on earth."

He couldn't imagine what she'd gone through, had to endure in silence. "Why didn't you tell your parents what was happening?" The two of them were anchored in the same grief. While he mourned for the deaths of his fiancées as well as the babe he'd never had, she mourned for her own child, her failed marriage, her broken dreams.

"How could I? They were living for Sybil, had all their hopes pinned on her. The beautiful seventeen-year-old would save them by making an advantageous marriage." Bitterness threaded through her voice. "I couldn't bring my shame or scandal to their doorstep and ruin my sister's chances."

When he would have gone to her, offered whatever comfort she would let him, Adriana held up a staying hand. "Let me finish, for once I break, I won't be able to tell you the rest."

"All right." Damn if he didn't hold the utmost respect for her but at the same time, he wanted to dig up the bastard who had hurt her and kill him all over again.

"After I lost the babe, Dan ignored me for a long while. In addition to his drinking, he began frequenting brothels, getting off his jollies there, and I was glad, for that meant he left me alone." She wiped the moisture on her cheeks. "There was nothing left between us, and that tiny hope I'd had—for my marriage, for love, for the babe—was gone. I was merely existing, waiting, wondering when the torture would end."

Needing to do something, Montague moved to a credenza where several cut crystal decanters of various spirits were stored. "How did his death come about?" He poured a measure of brandy into two crystal glasses, then crossed the room and pressed one of them into her hand.

"He was well into his cups one evening. It was raining but a warm June night. I'd been reading, and that had apparently enraged him. Dan yanked me from the sofa, threw the book at me." Adriana closed her eyes as she took a sip of the brandy. A wince crossed her face and twin spots of high color blazed on her pale cheeks, and she gave into a shiver. "He smacked me around, tore at my clothes, shoved me onto the sofa and tried to rape me."

Montague drifted closer to her. After downing the contents of his glass in one swallow, he rested it on the mantel and touched her shoulder. Her eyes flew open but were clouded with such agony, his heart squeezed. "Tell me the rest," he commanded in a voice graveled with emotion.

"I didn't want him, hadn't wanted him for a long time in any way, but he refused to leave off, even after I'd pleaded, told him no." She took another sip of the spirits. "I wasn't thinking, only reacting at that point. I grabbed a brass candlestick from the side table. It was one of a pair we'd received on our wedding day, one of the only things of value we had left. Once I'd scrambled to my feet, I swung it at him, used it as a weapon. Caught him on the side of his head." She stared at him with wide eyes and tears streaming down her face. "He sort of crumpled at that point. There was blood in his hair. It wet his cheek, and he fell to his knees but was up immediately and came after me."

Dear God. Montague removed the glass from her hand, put it on the windowsill. Satan promptly jumped up beside it and stuck his face into the glass. It would serve him right if he came away tipsy. Damned nosy cat.

"I retreated into the bedroom and slammed the door. He left in a rage shortly afterward. I heard his heavy footsteps on the treads in the corridor then saw him on the street below." Her words came fast and furious. They tripped over themselves in her haste to have the tale done with. "I don't know if he was nearly dead at that point from the blow I'd given him, or if he was merely disoriented, but he staggered into the path of an ongoing carriage. The driver couldn't stop in time. Dan was trampled by the horses." She scrubbed at her cheeks. "He lay there in the street, motionless, with his face and upper chest mangled."

There was nothing he could say, so Montague simply bundled his wife into an embrace and held her close. At first, she resisted, her body taut, but he refused to release her. Eventually, she relaxed into his care and sagged against him, sobbing.

He cleared his throat. "Was there an official inquiry?"

"Yes, of course, for a titled lord had been driving the carriage." Her words were slightly muffled from his clothing as she clung to him with her arms around his middle. "I told them exactly what I'd told you about what had occurred prior to the accident."

"And?"

"Their investigation was finished a few days later as inconclusive. The coroner ruled that Dan had died instantly from being struck by the horses' hooves and his ribcage crushed, his lungs punctured. Even had he not died in the street, he would have succumbed at hospital."

"Then you didn't kill him."

"They cannot know that!" She pulled slightly away to peer into his face. Those moisture-spiked lashes, the watery brown eyes, that trembling chin worked at his undoing. All he wanted to do was protect her from further ills. "I hit Dan hard with that candlestick. He could have been well on his way to dying; the side of his head had a decent enough bloody dent. Perhaps I'd addled his brain enough that he wasn't thinking clearly in the street."

"Or he'd pickled his own brain that such an ending would have befallen him in any event." Wanting to comfort her, reassure her, but not knowing how, Montague led her over to the sofa she'd vacated earlier, sat, and then gently pulled her down with him. He tucked her securely against his side with an arm around her. "I am so sorry you were forced to endure what you did."

"The gossips soon caught wind of what I'd done, what had happened, and then my whole sordid tale fed that machine for months."

"Because it was easier to run with the idea of a murderess than realize the truth."

"Yes." She accepted his handkerchief. "In shame and scandal, I had no choice except to return home. My parents railed, Sybil cried unfairness, but in the end, they took me back."

"But never let you forget how much their kindness was costing the family or your sister's future chances," he surmised in a soft voice. "And, of course, their disappointment grew."

"Yes. That was three years ago."

Near the time when he'd lost the woman he would have wed, the mother of his child.

Adriana cried into the handkerchief. "I have failed in every way a woman can, Montague." When she half-turned into him, he wrapped the other arm around her. That faint, pleasing scent of lilacs teased his nose, and he rather enjoyed the warmth of her. "It's why I didn't want a man—one of many reasons—or why I never wished to marry again. I couldn't go through that again. Not any of it."

For the first time since they'd wed, he finally understood what drove her and why she'd been dead set against not only the union but of him. "Yet now you are my wife, married to what the gossips say is a beast of a man, and that no doubt terrified you."

"Yes." She dabbed at her eyes with the handkerchief. "Knowing what little I did about you, the last thing I wished for was another drunken, violent husband."

His chest tightened, not with anger but with empathy. "And my attitude didn't endear me to you in those first days." When she remained silent, he sighed. "I apologize for my actions. There are times when I'm not quite certain how to behave like a person let alone a decent one when my mind is wracked by grief and emotions that still feel all too raw."

"It does sneak up on a person when they're unawares, and then we become horrid versions of ourselves for defense, to push everyone away."

"For protection. Against our history."

"Yes."

For long moments, the only sound in the room was the crackling of the fire, her occasional sniffling, and the comforting drum of the rain upon the window glass.

"How do you feel now?"

She shrugged. "Marginally better. At least you know all of my sorry tale and can make future decisions based upon that."

No longer did he wish to send her to his property in Essex. His wife was a fetching woman when she allowed herself to be vulnerable and need him, and she was rather easy on the eyes and felt all too good in his arms when she was in a temper. "We shall see what happens." Could he allow the walls around his heart to come down long enough to invite her fully in even with the risk?

Adriana stirred against him. "We should really attend your friend's luncheon."

"No." He snorted. "Being here with you is more important than doing the pretty. He will understand, and besides, we shall see them both at the upcoming ball Witherbone is throwing later in the month.

It's his autumnal tradition."

"Do you attend every year?"

Heat seeped over his collar. "No, but I thought you might wish to."

She pulled back from him and stared at him as if she were seeing him for the first time. He rather enjoyed keeping her off kilter and at sixes and sevens. "Be careful, Pennington. You might just change your ways and shatter that image of the beastly recluse."

"Bah." But there was no longer a bite in the word.

"Thank you for the gift of your library. I am sorry I pried into your room days ago."

"Think nothing of it. You had every right." Little by little, he was coming to trust her, but that didn't mean anything. There was much healing ahead, and how could he let her in if he couldn't let go of the past?

When she pushed upward and bussed his cheek, he stared at her even as the beginning stages of arousal went through his shaft. "I appreciate that you listened to me and didn't lecture. That marriage was my mistake and I have learned from it, but I've also grown from it too."

"Helped along by parents who didn't care." Had those experiences forged her into the woman she needed to be, the countess she now was, so that she could survive a lifetime with him? He didn't know, but he suddenly didn't want a woman to have to *endure* him. But how to move past the raw terror of sharing his history and heartbreak with another person when for so long he'd been by himself?

Not quite ready for that next step, he cleared his throat. "Hand me the book of Keats' poetry. I shall read to you for a while." When she did as he requested, he encouraged her to recline on the sofa with her head resting in his lap.

Satan, apparently not content unless he was in the middle of every-thing, jumped on the sofa, made himself at home on Adriana's hip, and then promptly closed his eyes.

It was all too cozy and domestic, and damn him if he didn't like how that felt too. But he treasured the new understanding they'd reached and remained cautiously optimistic about where they were headed.

If he didn't manage to cock it all up.

CHAPTER ELEVEN

October 22, 1817

I T HAD BEEN four days since Montague had heard his wife's confession and the sordid tale of her history that had led her into scandal. Four days since they'd come to that understanding and new way forward in the library. Four days since he'd made the effort to spend time with her and not retreat into the beast he'd become in recent years.

And every moment of it had been surprisingly glorious.

When he didn't have duties to Parliament or business, he lingered at his townhouse, for a different reason than brooding as he'd done in months past. More often than not, they would ensconce themselves in the library and pass many pleasant hours there with the fire crackling and Satan trying his darndest to knock down piles of books or unravel various ribbons on her dresses. Half the time, they would give up and play with the cat until he grew tired.

His wife was an intelligent woman, knowledgeable in many subjects. She knew how to play chess and didn't give him quarter when routing him about the board. More often than not, those games ended, not in a checkmate, but because Satan stole a critical piece of the game and then would have to be chased down.

Montague taught her to play whist and faro. She faltered a few times, but never let him cheat once she'd gotten the gist of the games.

At times, he would read to her as she did embroidery handiwork in the drawing room before a fire, but more often than not, they retreated to the library. Was there anything better in life for a man than having a fire in the grate, rain at the windows, a cat in his lap, and a charming woman who chuckled at his jokes?

Sometimes she would read to him, and he adored the sound of her voice. Then he would read to her, even the thrilling gothic tales she liked so much that made him snort with derision.

Other times they would stroll through Hyde Park or visit the British Museum, where she exclaimed at the treasures contained therein. During those outings, he wished he could show her the world, merely to see the wonder and surprise through her eyes as she realized just how big everything was.

Truly, she'd been deprived of many things in her life, and she deserved every goodness.

At still other times, when he wished to enter society and show the *beau monde* how proud he was of his wife, he took her to the opera. When she cried at the drama being enacted on stage, he lost a piece of his heart to her one night, and that had been another turning point in their relationship. No other woman in recent memory had been able to accomplish that in years since he'd entered seemingly a lifetime of grief.

Now, as his belly was full from an excellent dinner and his brain was pleasantly buzzed from the wine he'd had with his roast beef, Montague sat in the drawing room behind his easel while Satan poked about his paints and got more on his fur than anything else. Adriana had taken a book into her lap, but more often than not, she would glance out the window where the shadows of the night were gathering, and a dreamy expression came over her face as she woolgathered.

While she was distracted, he painted her portrait, for she was made for canvas even if she wasn't classically beautiful. Or perhaps *because* of it. She was a Raphaelite's dream, with curves and pink flesh and rich brown eyes strewn with stars. And in a gown of navy silk that had tiny silver glass beads sewn all over the fabric, she looked as if she'd fallen from the heavens.

As he glided his brush over the canvas in the hopes of portraying the exact way she held her head as well as the precise curve of her cheek, his thoughts flitted to his alter ego. Should he tell her he was indeed one of her favorite modern artists? It was a daring notion, indeed, and it might bring her to a new understanding of him.

For the last four days, he'd wanted to tell her of his history like she'd done with him, wished to unburden himself of the terrible feelings of grief and loss, to ask if she would help him carry that weight for a time while he regained his strength.

Would she want to, or would she consider him weak and unworthy?

"Adriana?"

"Hmm?" She quit her contemplation of the world outside the window, and when she met his gaze, a soft smile curved her lips. Damn, but he hadn't kissed her delectable mouth since that night in the carriage. The taste and feel of it had haunted his dreams ever since.

"Do you remember when you told me that you admired the work of Monsieur René Depardieu?" He shooed Satan away from his paints, but not before the cat appropriated one of his skinnier brushes. The feline ran off with his prize. He'd lost more brushes and even pens to the furry thief over the years.

"Yes. Why?" Tendrils of blonde hair clung to her cheeks, and one even was curled tight into a ringlet at her nape. It never failed to stoke his interest, and in that moment, he wanted nothing more than to kiss that exact spot.

"Uh… I *am* that painter."

"What?" She stared at him with wide eyes. "Is that true or are you joking?"

"It's quite true." He turned his easel and canvas about so she could see. Though it was his wife reclining on a sofa, he'd chosen to paint her against a backdrop of ancient Greece with her clad in a tunic that fell in graceful lines about her form. "Shortly after the death of my second fiancée, I began to paint professionally, and not wishing to use my name, I made up the name of a French painter."

"That's… incredible," she breathed as she left the sofa and came closer.

"What, my news or my painting?" Oddly enough, he craved her praise and admiration.

"Both." Then wariness crept into her expression. "Those portraits in your dressing room… No wonder they looked familiar. You painted them. As René."

"I did. The name means 'born again' in French. I thought it fitting." He wiped the paint off his fingers onto a rag the best he could. "It was the only way I knew how to cope with loss and grief." The longer Adriana stared at the canvas, the more worried he grew. "Please say something."

"The way you managed to make something beautiful—many beautiful things—out of the tragedy your life had become is amazing." When she glanced at him and he spied the delight dancing in her eyes, he relaxed by increments.

"There is a certain order in painting. Yes, it is based in creativity, but there is a way it must be done to provide the effects I need."

"Will you please tell me about the paintings in your dressing room? Specifically, the ones that have a slash of red through them?"

Ah, God. Though he'd hoped she might broach the subject, he hadn't been as mentally prepared to go there as he'd thought. The tightness in his chest returned. Suddenly, he couldn't breathe. "No."

He pushed off his stool so quickly that it toppled over and clattered onto the floor. What he wanted most was to growl until she left his presence, to retreat into himself, to hide away until the ache from the pain died down, and as he edged toward the door, Adriana was there with a staying hand on his arm.

"Montague, don't go backward. I told you about my past, let you see my emotions even though they were raw and I hurt." She peered up at him with nothing but honesty and hope in her dark eyes. "Won't you do the same for me?"

"I... I..." He couldn't bear the inevitable pity in her expression despite getting along well right now. "Do not follow me." Unwilling to put himself into a position where that pain would become all-consuming, he departed the drawing room. She would think him broken and weak, and then disappointment would shadow her eyes, and it would leave him more shattered than he already was.

With each step, his chest ached, his heart squeezed. He couldn't properly breathe, and no sooner had he reached the relative safety of his dressing room, when Adriana followed him inside. Of course she did, because why wouldn't she? The woman never had followed orders.

When Tremaine poked his head into the room with a question, Montague snarled and dismissed him, then he rounded on her.

"I told you not to follow me."

She propped her hands upon her hips, which only served to call his attention to the flare of them and how he'd not gotten them quite right on the canvas downstairs. "I believe I told you some days ago that I'm your wife and we need to go through things together." When he said nothing but tried to move around her, she stepped into his path. "Sharing doesn't only go one way, Pennington. We are either in this marriage fully or not at all."

Why was she so... managing? He both liked it and loathed it, but she was quite correct. Adriana deserved some sort of explanation and recitation of his history. The servants and staff could have only indulged her curiosity so far.

"Fine!" Anger propelled that one word out on a roar. The heat of embarrassment quickly rose through his chest, for he hadn't meant for such a display. If she wanted the whole, sorry story, she would have it. Successfully maneuvering around her this time, he went to the first collection of paintings, pulled one after the other out and stacked them on the floor. Some of them went back three years. "Some of these women were my mistresses. Some of the portraits were merely of daring, bored women who'd wished for the scandal of being painted nude."

"Why did they come to you?"

"Because I am good at what I do." He couldn't help the note of arrogance in his voice. "And I'd made myself into the worst man in London, remember?" After a shrug, he threw two more portraits onto the pile. "Besides, I adore the craft too much to turn down paid commissions." Another swath of anger swept through him. He smashed one of the paintings over a knee, threw the broken, twisted canvas aside while she cringed. "None of these helped fill the void inside or stopped the pain. Neither did taking the women into my bed."

As if the act of talking about it had flipped a switch inside him, more and more words welled into his being, lined up and waited their turn to be set free.

"Nothing can ever take away that pain," he admitted in a low voice, forced through his throat tight with unshed tears.

Not once had he talked about the deaths of his fiancées with anyone. The bulk of London society merely knew that they had died, but not how much the loss of those women had affected him on a deeply personal level. After all, weren't English peers supposed to keep a stiff, upper lip at all times, act as though nothing bothered them, for they had schedules to keep?

"And quite frankly, I'm tired of trying to hold in the pain." He took up another painting, ripped at the canvas, peeled it off the frame and then tossed the whole lot to the floor.

"Then let it out, Pennington. It's past time." Adriana moved to the other side of the room. She pulled out one of the portraits that had a red slash through it.

God, he remembered the day in a rage he'd taken out his carnelian paint and using his fattest brush, had slashed the perfection of that painting as well as its companion piece, for gazing upon them had only made the pain increase, the grief intensify.

"Tell me about her," she asked softly as she propped the canvas against the clothespress.

"Lady Catherine." Montague glanced at the portrait. "We'd met at a ball, and as silly as it sounds, it was love at first sight." He shrugged, kicked at the stack of portraits he'd assembled and came closer to the painting and his wife. "I was a cocky, arrogant earl of thirty; she had made her Come Out the year before, but I was enchanted."

"She *was* quite lovely."

"Agreed. After six weeks, I asked for her hand. We were engaged and soon planning to wed as soon as the banns were read, for why wait?" He trained his gaze on the blue-eyed brunette who smiled back at him despite the thick red slash through the portrait. "But I was never given the opportunity to marry her."

"Why?"

"One afternoon, we'd planned to meet in Hyde Park before going on to an event that evening. She'd moved ahead of her maid—the girl had an issue with a boot lace if I recall—and in that short amount of time, Catherine was set upon by a vagrant." The pain that ricocheted through his chest as he told the tale stole his breath, made him slightly dizzy. "By the time I had arrived on the scene, she had already lost so much blood from the five knife wounds in her chest there was nothing I could do except hold her as she died."

"Merciful heavens." Adriana laid a hand on his arm. "So that's why you dislike Hyde Park or me going there alone."

"Yes." He bit off the reply before he could order her from the room as he wished to—before he could hide. Then he snatched up the portrait. "I should have destroyed this long ago. It only serves as a remembrance of what I don't have, of my failure to protect her."

When he would have smashed it, Adriana took hold of the frame and wrenched it from his hands. "This is a precious piece of your past. It is a beautiful piece of a beautiful woman—a woman you once loved. Do not destroy it while you are under high duress."

"But I've ruined it." Breathing heavily, he collapsed to his knees, burying his face in his hands lest she see too much of his soul.

"It's not. Especially when you remember Catherine the way she was in your heart, the way she made you feel, and how much you loved her." Adriana set the canvas against the far wall, out of his reach. "Perhaps we can have the portraits restored, after a time." She brought out the other painting. "Tell me about Rachel."

How the devil had she discovered the names of the women, he would never know, but it didn't matter. "I…"

"Tell me about the babe." Her voice broke on the last word, and he pressed a hand to his heart. In this moment, they were both still grieving.

The only difference was now they did so together. It made a difference. So much so that he gasped for breath.

Montague rubbed the heels of his hands into his eyes before finally looking at the painting. Damn, but she'd had the most piercing green eyes he'd ever seen, and her hair had been the color of chestnuts. "I'd waited an inordinate amount of time after Catherine's death to become marriage-minded once more."

"That's understandable." She rested that canvas next to the first.

"Ashbury prodded me to put myself back out there, to find happiness again."

"He sounds like a clever individual if he bullied you into that."

Though a faint grin tugged at the corners of his mouth, Montague couldn't keep the tears from welling in his eyes. It seemed once he'd started talking, he was unable to stop, and he wanted his wife to hear it all, to understand what had made him into such a growling, snapping beast. To help him out of it. "Three years ago, a fever had swept through London. I didn't think anything of it at the time because I was consumed by her, having just been engaged and floating from the news that she was with child."

A spasm went across Adriana's face. Did she recall her own time, her own hope? "I remember that. Some people said it was brought back with soldiers returning from the war."

"It matters not. Both Rachel and I contracted it, and along with it was an ailment that affected the lungs." In his mind, he remembered the horrible pressure that had been in his chest as he'd tried to breathe, of the sound of Rachel's labored breathing there at the last. "After a few weeks, I was well on the mend, so I called at Rachel's house to check on her."

"Oh, no." When Adriana would have moved away, he caught her hand.

"Where I had grown better, she had taken a turn for the worse." His voice cracked, broke. "Perhaps carrying the babe had weakened her body, but she was never strong enough to recover." Tears ran unchecked down his cheeks.

"You needn't continue if it causes you too much distress." Tears sparkled in his wife's eyes, and in that moment, he was so grateful to have her.

"Let me finish. I'm nearly at the end." Finally talking about this, though painful, would hopefully prove cathartic. "I can still hear that horrible rattle of her last breaths. I held her hand as she closed her eyes for the last time." A sob tore from his throat, for remembering, speaking about the past ripped through him and shredded him anew.

"That time I knew my heart would never recover, and I vowed to give it out no longer. It's too hard to come back from grief."

"I'm so sorry, Montague." She touched her free hand to his head, furrowing her fingers through his hair. "But if you don't allow your heart to function, are you truly living or merely existing?"

Damn, that slight hope at the backs of her eyes sent guilt deep into his chest. "It's frightening to contemplate." He turned into her, pressed his face into her belly while holding onto her legs as if she alone were his lifeline. "I lost my family that terrible winter day, Adriana." The agony in his voice was evident to his own ears. "More than anything I wanted that child, that chance, but fate didn't let me." Sobs racked his body and he cried into the rounded softness of her. "I shattered that day. My heart was gone, my dreams dashed, my strength stolen."

The rhythmic stroking of her fingers through his hair worked to bring a modicum of calm back to him. "And you hid from the world, burying yourself into the worst vices of society so no one would see your pain or pity you."

"Yes." It was nice to have someone about who understood. He shook from the force of his emotions that had suddenly been unleashed. Knowing he'd told her his history, he rocked from that shock, but it was oddly somewhat of a relief to have it out, as if he might not feel compelled to carry it all the time anymore. "I loved them, Adriana. Loved them with everything I was, and that wasn't enough to keep them with me." *I cannot do that again.* "Now you know why I cannot give you my heart."

Except, he was beginning to suspect that wasn't entirely true. Over the past week or so, he had come to enjoy having her about and trying to make her smile, learning about her as well as verbally sparring with her. Though he hadn't attempted a kiss since that night in the carriage, that desire for her hadn't faded, and sometimes it was all he could do to not carry her upstairs, but he didn't want to traumatize her after what she'd told him.

Because of that, would she eventually leave?

When he expected his wife would rail at him or at the very least bedevil him about his decision, another wave of shock plowed into him when she instead sobbed alongside with him. "I understand. Please do not think that I don't, but don't discount how lovely love can be. It can help you heal." Adriana put her hands on either side of his head, tilted it upward until their gazes connected. "Truly, I am sorry though that I cannot be what you want—what you need—because I am broken too."

What the devil? "That's not what I meant—"

"Of course it is. I can see it in your eyes, in your face when you don't think anyone is looking. I know that longing, too." She shook her head. A few tears dropped onto his cheek. "You can possibly find love and romance with someone more suitable a few years from now once I am no longer a hinderance."

"What?" Her words sobered him, chased away some of the sadness. Clarity returned with a trace of annoyance. "What are you saying?" Her words were entirely too ominous and much like she would abandon their marriage.

Desolation lined her expression. "You are a good man deep down, Pennington, but were merely lost for a while." In the attempt to stifle a sob, she uttered a weird hiccupping sound. "And I…" The tendons in her throat worked with a hard swallow. "I will remain unwanted, unappreciated, and ultimately unloved for what I am not, for what I can never achieve. For what you desperately wish for."

Then, with a heartbreaking wail, Adriana pulled away, out of his arms, and fled the room as if she couldn't bear to linger in his company.

CHAPTER TWELVE

*H*E WILL NEVER *love me as he loved them.*

Adriana had suspected but it hadn't hit home for her until he'd told her the secrets of his heart and how his pain from loss had affected him. Montague had loved his previous fiancées so much that he'd given them all of him, everything that he was, but he couldn't—wouldn't—do the same for her.

To say nothing of the fact that he wanted an heir—or simply a child—that he'd mourned hard for the death of his unborn babe just as she had for hers, but that was the one thing she couldn't do for him. She couldn't conceive a child, and because of that, what use was she? What value had she if she was unable to fulfill that dream for them both?

A sob escaped as she gained the privacy of her rooms. Since marrying Montague, her emotions had been at sixes and sevens over one thing or another. He was big and intense, and his grief, his anger fed her own, but if neither of them funneled that energy into something productive, they would burn each other out. One couldn't be healed if the other remained jagged.

Or drive each other away.

But oh, she'd had a tiny niggle of a dream during the last halcyon days she'd spent with her husband when she'd had a chance at everything she'd ever wanted… until his admission had shown her starkly she would never be that for him. Once again, she had disappointed someone in her life, and this one hurt with the accuracy of being stabbed.

She couldn't bear it this time, not with him, not when there had been *something* shared between them that hadn't been present those first days of their marriage.

Again, she felt as if she were drowning. Not in him but in another wave of grief, this time for something possibly sweeter than she'd ever had before.

When would it end? When would she forgive herself for the things that weren't her fault, that she had no control over?

To accept herself as she was?

After hearing the earl's story, she'd come to a startling decision: she had to set him free.

"Adriana." Pennington came into the bedchamber, for she'd neglected to close the door.

"Go away." Her tears came all the harder as she pressed her face into the counterpane. A family would restore his faith in love and romance, in fate and humanity. It would heal his heart and make him happy, but it was also the one thing that was beyond her power.

"I won't do that, but I must say I'm growing weary of having to chase you down because you've fled." The trace of humor in his voice caused her chin to tremble, but she ignored him the best she could. "I want to help."

"You cannot." She sniffled. "No one can. Please leave."

"Let *me* decide what I can and cannot do." His voice sounded all too close, and when she lifted her head, she gasped, for he was at her bedside. Seconds later, the earl scooped her into his arms as if she weighed nothing. He carried her over to a wing-backed chair and then sat with her cradled in his lap like a babe. "Tell me why you said what you did just now."

Oh, he wouldn't understand. "I cannot—"

"You can." His voice had dropped and was so soft that it sent tingles of anticipation down her spine. "Since you bedeviled my secrets from me, I wish to do the same for you." When she didn't respond, he fit his lips to the shell of her ear. "And just a warning. I don't play fair."

She tamped down a shiver. "Meaning?"

He chuckled. "I'm not above employing seduction to help my cause."

Mercy. Awareness enveloped her. Being this close to him swamped her system, made her want to burrow deep into his arms and stay there, let him protect her. "You are a cheater, Pennington."

"Never." Montague stroked a hand up and down her arm. "Why are you afraid of our marriage all of a sudden? I had thought we'd reached a new understanding in our relationship." He sounded genuinely confused.

Sometimes, he was a dear man. A puzzle to be solved, certainly, but in many ways, he was the rational side she needed at times. "You will surely hate me."

"I couldn't." He nuzzled his nose into her hair. "Unless you plan to thwack me upside the head with a candlestick. We only have silver in this house, and I know that's not your preference…"

"Pennington!" She squealed in mock outrage, but his teasing had provoked a smile from her. With a sigh, Adriana rested her head on his chest. "You haven't grown that much in the short time I've been with you."

"Tell me." Up and down his fingers danced on her arm. "I have no right to pass judgment on any of your decisions." He maneuvered his head so their gazes connected. "You never did with me."

"True." It was rather enjoyable being with him like this. Almost as if he might cherish her, but that was a silly thought. "I told you a handful of days ago I had the dream of a child."

"Yes." The man didn't prod or rush her, and for that, she appreciated him all the more. "You told me that you'd lost the baby."

"I did, but there were circumstances surrounding that event which haunt me."

"Such as?" Wariness had crept into his voice.

Sooner or later, he would see her for the pathetic creature she truly was. "Oh, I was cautiously happy, Montague." She fiddled with the folds of his cravat. "Finally, I would have someone in my life who would need me, want me, love me unconditionally." Tears welled in her eyes. "I couldn't begin to hope at that time, but I knew I was with child, having missed two menses. A woman just feels differently."

"Did you visit a midwife?"

"There was no time." She never got to enjoy that wonderful feeling.

"What happened?"

The rhythmic touch of his fingers on her arm both calmed and aroused. What she wouldn't give to tumble into bed with him, ask him to do all sorts of naughty things to her so that she might forget for one moment... "One night, I told Dan about my suspicions, that I would make an appointment with a midwife to confirm so we could start to plan. And in that way perhaps he would work harder on making an income."

Montague snorted. "From everything I've heard about this bounder, I don't think even having a child would have made him sober." He held her a tad closer. "Was your husband a proper jubilant father-to-be?"

"Not in the slightest." Tears fell to her cheeks in a hot stream. When he pressed his handkerchief into her hand, she sighed. He was as different from Dan as day was to night. "My husband was enraged when I told him. That night he was halfway into his cups, of course." She sniffled. "Said it was another mouth to feed, another responsibility while business was already strained." The feelings from that terrible time came flooding back, and in lieu of curling into a ball and sobbing for the next three days, Adriana clung to him.

"What did he do?" the earl asked in a small, tight voice. "Though I can suspect…"

Best to tell him the rest quickly, for it wasn't pleasant. "He beat me that night. One of the worst I'd ever received, made certain to contain his blows to my belly, my sides."

"Bloody hell." When she glanced up into his face, there was shock in his eyes.

"Of course, I lost the babe. Two days later." She could barely force the words from her tear-crowded throat. "That was when *my* heart withered, and *my* dreams died."

"How long after that did your husband die?"

"About six months."

"Did you come together carnally in that time?"

"Yes. Twice by my consent. I'd hoped, stupidly now, for a connection or for support, but it wasn't there. Dan didn't care about me as a woman, as a grieving parent. I was foolish and didn't conceive again."

"And the rest of that story I already know. You'd reached a breaking point and essentially changed your fate."

"I suppose."

For long moments, Montague was silent. "I'm so sorry, sweeting." Had he meant to use the endearment? "It's a horrid tale to be sure. If Dan was alive, I would have called him out, demand that he face me on a dueling field."

"He was too stupid and too drunk to wield a pistol, but thank you."

"Then let me now utter the question that has been eating at me. Why did you flee from me again? Why did you tell me to find someone to love as if you are suddenly gone from this union."

She took in a ragged breath. "I cannot give you the heir—or even a child—that you desire. I saw the look in your eyes, Montague. You were already in love with that babe you lost. That is something I can never gift you with, and I don't want to spend the rest of my life knowing I've disappointed you or that you have grown to resent me."

"I rather doubt that will come to pass. There is more to life than children."

No doubt he only said that as empty comfort. "I am sorry for trapping you into this union. It wasn't fair, to either of us."

"You only played a small part in that. I lay the blame of the whole thing at Mrs. Dove-Lyon's feet." When he nudged her ear with his nose, she couldn't help but giggle. "But what is not fair is you feeling less than because of what you are not." Pennington cupped her cheek, tilted her head back until their gazes connected. "Why can you not see what I am beginning to regarding you?"

Dear heavens. What did that mean? She didn't dare to hope. "But—"

"Ah, Adriana. It seems I am not the only one hiding behind old ideals and outdated notions out of fear." He pressed his lips to her temple. "It is much too early in our union to declare defeat when we haven't yet begun to fight. Together. *For* each other."

Did that mean he was fully committed to the marriage? She didn't dare ask. "Yes, but—"

"Hush." He chuckled and the sound reverberated deep in her chest with the most delicious tingles. "Rest your mind. Know that you are safe and that I am not disappointed in you." Tenderly, he brushed at the lingering moisture on her cheek. "Some of the burdens weighting us down have fallen away after what we shared tonight. Let us rejoice in that."

"I would be happy to talk more if you wish it." Had she truly helped him? It made her feel almost giddy that someone had relied on her, depended on her.

"Perhaps another time. One is not healed so soon after bearing one's soul, I think." Then he shifted her slightly in his embrace and claimed her lips in a gentle kiss that had need flaring more than it comforted.

Oh, it would be so easy to lose herself in this man—to fall in love with him—if she would just let it happen. But there were so many unknowns, and the future was far from settled. A man could put on his best behavior in order to win whatever he wanted, and then show his true colors once it was too late. She had to remain careful.

With a shuddering sigh, Adriana kissed him back. She'd missed that so much since the night of the carriage ride, missed that swift carnal connection between them, and beyond that missed the warmth and closeness they'd begun to build.

Before things could turn interesting, he pulled away. "It has been a tiring evening." When he urged her off his lap, she uttered a protest, but then he picked her back up into his arms and carried her across the floor to the bed. "You need rest," he murmured as he laid her upon the counterpane. He was easily the most handsome man as he leaned over her, and the candlelight provided shifting shadows over his face. "Shall I ring for your maid?"

"No." She clung to his hand. Still vulnerable from baring the re-mainder of her soul to him, she didn't want their time together to end. "Stay with me, Montague." When his eyes widened, she nodded. "Just for tonight. I'd rather not be alone, and perhaps you might feel the same?" When he hesitated, she smiled. "It doesn't mean I love you, in the event you wondered." Would he realize she'd used the same words he'd said to her on that night?

"Minx. I understand." But he blew out the candle on the bedside table. A few seconds later, the unmistakable thuds of his boots hitting the floor echoed in the darkness. Then he'd joined her, and she was tucked beneath him, and his lips were at the side of her neck, his hands going beneath her skirts. "I suppose it's only right to assist you out of this gown."

"Now who's the cheeky one?" With a sigh, Adriana gave herself into his care. She hadn't planned on being intimate with him tonight, for she'd merely wanted his company, to feel his solid weight and warmth next to her in the bed, but this was infinitely better.

At the back of her mind, she knew this would never work, for he required an heir. Neither of them could deny that, but perhaps it didn't matter. In this moment, there was only her and him, and they'd made great strides at growing closer this evening.

She could meet everything else as it came before her courage fully deserted her.

Hopefully.

CHAPTER THIRTEEN

October 25, 1817

MONTAGUE'S HANDS SHOOK as he manipulated the gold fastening at Adriana's nape. It was all he could do not to press his lips to that spot where that little blonde curl beckoned. He'd gifted her the emerald necklace that matched her wedding ring, for they would leave for Witherbone's ball in mere moments, and he'd wished to give her something, anything, that would show her he wasn't merely the beast he thought, or the man trapped by grief unable to give away his heart.

"There." He guided her over to the cheval glass in her dressing room. Behind him on a sofa, Satan was engaged in a vigorous cleaning of his feline form. "The emeralds seem made for you." Five square-cut emeralds of four-carats each reposed in a gold setting. Smaller round diamonds connected each emerald together. The whole lot sparkled in the candlelight. With her hair upswept and arranged into an elaborate coif of curls and braids, all held in place with pins and glittering golden combs, the necklace would call attention to her neck and décolletage. "Do you like it?" The colors went well with her gown of saffron silk, and the rich hue practically dared everyone to look at her, notice her.

Adriana touched the necklace with a gloved fingertip, but her gaze wasn't on the bauble. She looked at him through the mirror. "It's wonderful. You didn't need to gift this to me."

"Oh, but I did." He was on the verge of making a cake of himself, for the past three days had been nothing short of wonderful. "You are worth these and so much more." Only the fact that she would berate him had stopped Montague from delving into his safe and showering her with other jewels as an effort to show her how much she was beginning to mean to him.

Ever since she'd invited him into her bed that night after they'd shared their heartache and pain, some of the walls about his heart had crumbled and fallen. For the first time in three years, he had let himself hope, let himself dream she might be what he'd been looking for in this stage of his life, that she was exactly what he needed. She was strong and forthright, intelligent and beguiling, didn't give a fig for what society thought, and she wouldn't let him bully her when he lashed out due to pain or anger.

In her, he finally saw that he could build a life together with another person, and it didn't matter what that life looked like right now, for it had glorious potential.

And damn his eyes but he craved that companion, and dare he say love?

Did she love him?

At times during the past three days when he'd glanced at her, her expression had held such softness, her eyes twinkled with a secret he wasn't a part of, and he would venture a guess that she did, but she hadn't spoken about it, hadn't shared that revelation with him.

Was she as wary as he? Did she fear having her heart broken and her dreams shattered again? He couldn't blame her after the history she'd survived.

But I am not like that, will never treat her like that.

How much longer would it take before he could convince her?

Convince himself, perhaps?

"It's a pretty piece," she finally said and offered him a smile that had the power to warm him and tingle through his stones. Then she smoothed her hands along the front of her frock. "As is the gown. I've never worn such beautiful things."

Heavy beadwork lined the bodice; the tiny beads of clear glass and gold glittered with her every movement. A matching band of the same went about the high waist and another lined the hem. The sleeves ended at her elbows tied with delicate bows, and the matching emerald bracelet twinkled from her wrist.

"You are every inch a countess to be proud of, to be admired." Emotion graveled his voice, and he suspected he was seconds away from becoming a fool in front of her. Gently, he turned her away from the cheval glass and held her in a loose embrace. "*My* countess."

Damn, but that felt all too good speaking aloud.

"Oh, Montague." Adriana cupped his cheek, and it took all his willpower to tamp down the urge not to nuzzle into her palm, or to carry her into his bedchamber and spend copious moments removing that gown from her person merely so he could peruse her body at his leisure. "You are a dear, dear man. I will never forget the time spent in your company."

What was this, then? When he peered more closely into her eyes, sorrow lurked deep in those depths. But why? Hadn't they reached a new place in their union that they could move forward together? A chill of foreboding twisted up his spine. "Why do I have the feeling you haven't told me everything?"

Or more to the point, that she had made plans and excluded him from them.

"There is nothing about me that you don't already know." She lifted onto her toes, slipped her hand to his nape, and guided his head to hers. "I would also caution that you spend entirely too much time thinking." Then she kissed him, and he was lost to a sea of emotion he didn't dare analyze at the moment.

Once she pulled away, he stared at her, but those shadows in her eyes hadn't fled. "Do you still wish to attend this ball?" It was the first time they would appear in society as a married couple. "If you are anxious—"

"No." She rested a hand on his chest. "We should go. I wish to dance with you, so that I can always remember what it felt like, to know that I had a glimpse of perfection for a tiny moment in time." Abruptly, she pulled away and crossed the floor to the door, but not before he heard the unmistakable sound of a stifled cry. "Come, Pennington. We shouldn't dawdle."

What the hell? He frowned as she left the room, and that damned tingle of foreboding returned with a vengeance. "I am not the only one who is overthinking at the moment," he told Satan, who looked back at him with inscrutable green eyes. "She is quite maddening."

The cat uttered a meow, but he glanced at the door where Adriana had disappeared.

"I know. But how do I convince the woman she is enough? That I want her above everything instead of what she can give me or not?" That was the crux of the problem, he would wager the contents of his coffers on it. She was torturing herself with her inability to reproduce.

None of it mattered, not when he was inordinately happy to have his wife.

Satan meowed again, and Montague snorted.

"Why do you assume *I* will cock things up?" Shaking his head, he left the room, but the worry wouldn't leave him.

AN HOUR LATER, he stood with a flute of champagne in hand as he talked with Lord Ashbury while Adriana held court inside a small circle of both men and women.

"Careful, Pennington, else you'll burst with pride," the viscount cautioned with more than a little amusement in his voice.

"Do shut up." He took a sip of the sparkling wine, but his gaze never left his wife. Why had he fought so hard against the marriage? This was nothing like he imagined it would be, and in many ways, it had become rewarding over and above expectations. Then he slid his attention to his best friend. "In fact, I truly hope you land in the same muck I'm in, and soon, because even though this life is raw and emotional and at times horrid, it is also... wonderful."

Had he said too much?

Ashbury snorted. "Who are you and what have you done with the real Pennington? I rather miss the snapping beast I had for a best friend."

"Gammon." But Montague allowed a grin. It was odd, this giving himself permission to become a new person, all because of her, all *for* her. "Leave off with the teasing."

"Have you told her your history? Or have you locked yourself away, yelling her into submission?"

As if Adriana would ever allow anyone to have mastery over her. The thought had him chuckling, until Ashbury narrowed his eyes. "Yes. Bit by bit, but it's a difficult endeavor."

"It's supposed to be, for you are not an easy man to swallow." Speculation pooled in Ashbury's eyes. "Do you enjoy having a wife? It certainly seems so. You are fairly exuding contentment."

Heat crept up the back of his neck. "I don't know." Yet, he grinned. That alone was telling, so he hid the gesture behind the façade of taking another sip of champagne.

"Ah, I see." A cheeky grin curved the viscount's lips. "Have you had her in your bed?"

"Yes, and not in a bed as well," he couldn't help adding, just to make it maddening for his friend, but the heat on his neck intensified. The night Adriana didn't wish to be alone, he'd made love to her, and though it hadn't been as frantic or passionate as the time in the carriage, they had both had a lovely time.

Ashbury snorted. "Did you enjoy that?"

What sort of a nodcock question was that? "I'm not a monk, Thomas. Of course I enjoyed it, and I wouldn't continue to bed my wife if I didn't." For they'd come together again this morning. When he'd entered her suite to escort her to breakfast, she'd just stepped out of an enamel bathtub and had looked like a veritable Aphrodite.

Remembering that pleasant hour of exploration and pleasure had his shaft twitching in anticipation of another round.

"I see." Ashbury grinned like an idiot, but oddly enough, Montague didn't mind. "Are you connecting with your countess well enough in other areas of life beyond the bed sheets?"

"I would like to hope so." As he drained his glass, Montague took the time to analyze what exactly he felt for Adriana, and when he finished, he had no more excuses to deny it. He was falling—had fallen?—in love with his wife. When and how it had happened eluded him, for it had been such a gradual tumble that he hadn't realized it.

The question now was, did he have the courage to tell her, to formally offer her his heart knowing it would make him vulnerable a third time? Knowing there was something going on with her that still had the power to leave him cold with worry?

Since Ashbury waited on an answer, he sighed and set his empty flute on a silver tray that a passing footman held. "What if it all goes wrong? What if *I'm* wrong?"

"What if you aren't and it all goes right finally?" the viscount countered as his attitude sobered.

Montague snorted. Once more, his gaze went to Adriana, and damn if his heartbeat didn't skip. "How can it not? I've made myself into a monster—the worst man in London. I've kept people away to avoid living. Have I ruined everything?"

"Stop that, Pennington." Thomas slapped his shoulder. "You are not that man and we both know it. The odds of you having good fortune this third time are high. Why not give yourself permission to enjoy this?"

"I suddenly find my confidence is flagging. There are so many questions, worries…"

"Don't let them undermine what you are feeling." Shadows clouded his friend's eyes. "A successful marriage takes a concentrated effort, but I realize it's difficult letting go of the past." He drained his own glass. "I'm afraid I fail at that too. Many times over, and because of that have hurt my own chances to find what you currently have."

Despite having known this man for the bulk of his adult life, Montague frowned. What exactly had the viscount done in his romantic endeavors that left him envying his? "I want to try, keep trying, for Adriana. She is worth all the pain that might bring."

"Good." Ashbury gave himself a little shake. "That is wonderful progress for you, and something I never thought I'd see." Admiration slipped into his expression. "Does she return your budding feelings?"

"It is too early to tell."

The viscount snorted. "I think you can tell already. Hell, you are moony about her, but you are afraid of hoping in the event she's only wanted the physical from you, or is playing a game."

None of those thoughts had entered his mind, but now that they'd been given life, the muscles in his belly tightened with worry. "Perhaps." Again, his gaze strayed to her, and his heart squeezed when she laughed at something another woman had said. "She is challenging in the best ways. Accepting of me. I rather like having her about, have looked forward to spending time with her." He flicked his gaze back to Ashbury. "I let her have use of my library."

The viscount stared and his jaw dropped. "Damn, Pennington, that must be love." When Montague scoffed, Ashbury sailed on. "Let yourself complete the fall, my friend. Where is the harm? You are already wed, and things are apparently well."

He couldn't stop his grin. "Is it worth it, Thomas? Is love worth the pain? Will I truly find happiness, and have it stick this time?"

"Only you can say, but I certainly think love and romance is worth pursuing despite the risk and oftentimes high cost."

"Yet…"

"Yes?"

"Adriana is not capable of conceiving a child. There is no chance of an heir." It was the only fly in the ointment, but one he would overlook it if meant winning her heart. "Am I a failure if I don't do that duty to the title?"

"That is something only you can answer, but at times, there are more important matters than having children." He dropped a hand on Montague's shoulder and squeezed. "Has a physician confirmed that suspicion?"

"I don't believe so."

"Then be patient. Let yourself love her fully. Give her your heart. Enjoy the time with her, and then revisit the matter years from now."

"It weighs on her, puts sadness in her eyes. Holds her back." And he would do everything in his power to banish those feelings.

Because he loved her.

"Then make certain your wife knows that you care for *her*, that you want *her* instead of what she can do for *you*." A wicked glint appeared in the viscount's eyes. "Unless, of course, it is acts performed in the bedroom, then that is an entirely different conversation."

Montague couldn't help his guffaw even as the heat returned to his neck. "I am trying, Ashbury, but she has her own demons to fight."

"Help her in that, too. They won't suddenly vanish, for you have both lived a lifetime collecting them. I rather think it will take some time for the pair of you." The viscount's gaze went to Adriana. "Go dance with her or I will."

A swift stab of hot jealousy went through Montague's chest. "Not while I'm alive." Though she'd been quiet and withdrawn over the past few days, he would fight for the dream of them together. He wanted all of her, and if this current broken version of her was what she had to don in order to fight through her own thoughts, he would support her in it, offer protection should she want it. "If you will excuse me? They are setting up for a waltz."

"Best wishes, my friend. It is good to see you rejoining the living."

Except he couldn't shake the feeling that something horrible was still to come. By the time he'd led Adriana to an empty spot on the dance floor, the first notes of the waltz echoed through the air and didn't provide him with the opportunity to converse.

But every touch of their hands when she returned to partner him again, each time their gazes connected, the pull, the feelings he had for her grew until he was confidently certain he loved her. Despite the contention at the beginning of their union, he had discovered gold amidst the rocks he thought he'd been given. She'd arrived in his life with a mallet in hand and hadn't stopped knocking down the walls he'd erected until she could let in enough light that it began its cleansing process.

"You look as if you've just had an epiphany, Pennington," Adriana whispered when she came back to him in the steps of the dance.

"Perhaps I have." He couldn't help but grin, for she hadn't stopped poking and prodding until she'd dragged him out of the dark cave he'd consigned himself to. "Thanks to you."

A pretty blush stained her cheeks. "You would have figured it out eventually."

"I doubt that. I was two steps from becoming a hermit before you arrived."

She snorted, but her smile didn't reach her eyes. "But you aren't."

"Thanks to you." He held onto her fingers a tad too long than convention dictated, but then she moved away from him in the steps of the dance. What ailed her tonight? The second she returned to him, he held her closer than the movements demanded, but damned if he cared. This woman had changed everything for him, and he needed to tell her that. When the set came to an end, Montague put a hand to the small of her back and led her off the floor, not stopping until he'd ducked behind a grouping of potted ferns and other plants that acted much like a living shield. "Are you enjoying yourself this evening?"

"Yes, and in many ways, I wish it wouldn't need to end." If her voice hadn't wavered on that last word, if her chin hadn't wobbled, if there hadn't been a flash of sorrow in her dark eyes, he would have taken her words at face value. But he couldn't ignore those signs of distress.

"What is wrong?" When she didn't answer, his worry flared. And then he *knew*. She was going to leave him, abandon everything they'd worked toward this past two weeks or so.

And that terrified him.

In an effort to try and mitigate that inevitability, Montague took her into his arms, lowered his head, and claimed her lips. A tiny cry escaped her, but Adriana slipped her hands up his chest, looped her arms about his shoulders, and kissed him back with all the ardor he'd expected from her. He made love to her mouth as if he had all the time in the world and they weren't in an exceedingly public place in the hopes she would change her mind.

But, that perfect kiss couldn't last forever. Eventually, he pulled away and peered into her eyes, caught the sadness there, and his heart trembled. "You don't wish to be with me anymore." It wasn't a question. How could it be when her anguish was there and blocking her sight to all the good they could find together.

She shook her head. "I *must* set you free, Montague. Don't you understand?"

His world crashed down about his feet as she uttered those words. "Why? Things between us are growing better every day."

A tear fell to her cheek as she pushed out of his arms. "You need someone better than me. I was a ninny to think that we could have…" Her bottom lip quivered. She rested a hand on her chest, and his gaze dropped briefly to the tops of her breasts on display in that gown. "You need a woman who will give you everything you will eventually want."

"But I want *you*." Pain set up around his heart, vicious in that it was familiar.

The laugh she uttered lost its punch as she sniffled. "You only think that now, but when you look at the situation with common sense, through the eyes of duty and responsibility, you will change your mind." Tears sparkled in her eyes. "I don't want to be the one who will make you wonder years from now, and I won't hold you back. I refuse to see any affection you have for me die in small ways..."

Panic tore at his throat. "You are throwing away all the wonderful we've created for something you think *might* happen in the future?" How was any of this happening? Why couldn't he reach her?

"I must." Her chin trembled. "Now that you are not the beast you've made yourself into, now that you are changing, you have a chance at happiness. At fulfillment. At love." The poor dear's voice broke again.

"I can have that—have it now—with *you*, Adriana."

"No. You only think you do." She shook her head and another tear fell to her cheek, but surprise jumped into her eyes. "I've thought about nothing else for the past three days, and this is the best decision for us both."

"You're leaving, then?" His chest was so tight he could scarcely breathe, but short of carrying her off and locking her into his town-house until she came to her senses, he could do nothing about it.

"Yes."

Oh, God. "And do what?"

"Gain a divorce from the only person who has the power to fix this."

Damn and blast. Surely, she didn't intend to seek out the owner of the Lyon's Den! He felt much like a man who has received a mortal blow but hasn't realized that he should fall. "Will that make you happy?" Bloody hell but that pain in his heart would kill him this time around. *This is why I never wanted another woman in my life.*

The heartache was unbearable, yet there would be no closure, for he would still see Adriana about London.

"Yes?" A sob quickly followed the confusion in the answer. "Please don't make this more difficult than it has to be."

Anger speared through his chest. "You are the one who is making it difficult, Adriana. I am giving you *everything*, wish to offer you all of me to make our union work, while you are…" A muscle ticced in his cheek from the effort of clenching his cheek. "You are declaring defeat on me. On us."

"Oh, Montague." She scrubbed at the moisture on her cheeks. "Let me go. It's for the best. Truly, and will save you so much pain and agony in the future."

"You don't know that!" At the last second, he modulated his voice to a dull roar. But in the end, he hung his head. If it wasn't this day, it would be another. She was determined; he knew that about her. "I can deny you nothing." As his heart broke into a million pieces a third time, he knew without question that it would never heal again. "If you don't believe I can make you happy, then go, and God be with you."

"I…" Then, with another sob and so many emotions in her eyes that he couldn't isolate merely one, she took her skirting in her hands and she ran.

Away from him.

Away from their life together.

Away from everything either of them had ever wanted.

Montague rested a fist on the wall and tried to hide his face with the other as sorrow crashed over him again and again. *I am such a damned fool.* Perhaps there was no other recourse except to return home and rage about like the beast he likened himself to.

For, after all, without her, wasn't that all he had left?

CHAPTER FOURTEEN

A DRIANA BARELY HEARD the steady rain as it came down against the roof and sides of the sleek carriage as she curled onto her side on the squabbed bench. Sobs held her in their grip; her heart felt shredded and pummeled, for the most difficult thing she'd ever done was leave Montague and the life they could have had together.

But how could that life have worked when he would grow resentful of her and her inability to conceive a child, the heir he would desperately need sooner or later?

That would have brought more pain to them both than what she experienced now.

"Perhaps Mrs. Dove-Lyon will help," she whispered to herself, but the only answer was more intense rain. "She simply must."

Thirty minutes later, she was waiting once more in the ladies' parlor at the Lyon's Den gaming establishment. A spattering of raindrops marred her beautiful skirting. One trickled down her temple as she waited with taut muscles and the constant ache about her heart. Would the proprietress see her?

Finally, just as her nerves felt like shattering, the female escort returned and beckoned at her to follow.

Once more, Adriana was shown into a room deep in the heart of the Lyon's Den, and once more she was instructed to take a seat on one of the lavishly upholstered sofas in the room.

Fabric rustled as someone else came into the space. The unmistakable scent of jasmine filled the air. "Lady Pennington. What a surprise."

"Mrs. Dove-Lyon. Thank goodness." Relief poured over her as she glanced at the other woman. She didn't wear a veil this time, but since the room was plunged into shadow from the light of the one candle across the room, it was difficult to discern what she looked like.

"I must say I'm perplexed to see you again, for I had assumed once the general rockiness of your relationship ironed itself out, you and the earl would have been ensconced somewhere doing what married people do."

Heat suffused Adriana's cheeks. Oh, if only life were that simple. She could have happily let Montague court her, seduce her with poetry readings and the cozy fire in his library and his proclivity for pleasure in the privacy of their rooms. "I need your assistance."

"So I assumed, but engaging in a threesome isn't something I am interested in, Lady Pennington."

"No, that's not what I meant." If she wasn't such a coward who had fled from her own husband—when he *wasn't* a bounder—she would have protested any woman who might have wanted to be with Montague.

"Then perhaps you should explain." The widow moved behind her. There was the clink of crystal against crystal, then Mrs. Dove-Lyon returned and pressed a glass into her hand. A sniff revealed it was brandy. "For if it was me wed to Lord Pennington, I wouldn't leave his side until I'd been quite thoroughly pleasured for a good three months. It was one of the reasons I agreed to match you with him in the first place."

That distracted her. "Whyever for?"

"Your life up until the point you married Pennington was full of horror and tragedy." Mrs. Dove-Lyon shrugged as if that settled it. "You didn't properly know what it was like to be wanted for a woman in your own right, and I'd guessed you'd not been taught pleasure or given the same in your first marriage bed."

"Do stop. I almost wish you'd never let me take my sister's place, for then I would never have known… would have never come together with…" The heat spread to her whole face. She took refuge in sipping at the brandy, but the burn in her throat reminded her of the day that Montague had given her a taste of the same. Tears sprang to her eyes again. Really, since her nuptial ceremony, she'd had the bad habit of becoming a watering pot.

"I am waiting to hear the reason for your visit, Lady Pennington." A fair amount of urgency rang in the other woman's voice.

"Right." Finally, she sighed and glanced at the widow when she alighted on a chair across the furniture grouping. "I need for you to arrange a divorce for me, to put up the blunt as well as the influence required for such a thing."

"I beg your pardon?" Shock wove through the inquiry.

Adriana took another fortifying sip of brandy and welcomed the burn in her throat as a distraction from the unrelenting pain around her heart. "I wish to have you arrange for a divorce. I cannot, in good conscience, remain married to Montague."

"Why the devil would you want that?" The widow set her glass onto a table with a decided thud. "Pennington is quite the catch."

"I agree. He is, but just not for me." Conscious of the widow's stare upon her, she sighed. "I am not the one who will make him happy years from now."

"How can you know that?"

How can I not? "I am unable to conceive a child."

Mrs. Dove-Lyon huffed. "As I told you when we first met, having children does not determine your worth as a woman or a person."

"I am aware of that, but eventually, my husband will *require* an heir, and whether he talks of it or not, he wishes for a child. I've seen that evidence in his eyes." Her voice broke when she explained the situation. "That is not something I will be able to give him. Down the line, I don't want him to resent me, or for regret to steal the other joys I've found with him."

"So, you have made this decision *for* your husband. Without regard to what he wants or might need later. Without regard to anything, apparently." Annoyance wove through the widow's voice. "Men are not complicated creatures, Lady Pennington. What they say they want now is usually what they will always want."

She swallowed around a ball of tears in her throat. "You don't know him."

"Forgive me for being so blunt, but neither do you." When Adriana didn't answer, Mrs. Dove-Lyon went on. "Do you not love your husband?"

Did she? He had certainly changed since she'd met him, and he claimed it was all due to her. But love? Her soul shivered each time she was in his vicinity. "I am not quite certain."

"Ah, so you have become a liar since your marriage." The widow snorted. Drat the ever-present shadows and darkness that clung to the room, for Adriana couldn't see her face. "You would not be driven to this desperate pass if you weren't, Lady Pennington."

Was that true? "I am doing this *for* him."

"Why?"

"Montague deserves more."

"How do you know he doesn't have that now?"

"Because I know what I am and what he can be... with someone else."

"So, then according to you, he's too much of a mess that you have lost patience with him? You have given up on all you have built together with him?" There was no trace of accommodation in the widow's voice.

Adriana sighed. "No. I am giving him the freedom of options."

"Did he ask for any of that? Did he specifically tell you he wanted a wife who could bear him a handful of children?"

"No, but surely every titled man has that dream." Didn't they?

"I am disappointed in you, Lady Pennington, for I assumed you were made of sterner stuff than this. I thought you were more intelligent."

"Yes, well, I have a long list of people I have disappointed." Except Montague. He never seemed that way with her, had never said the words, had never even looked that way at her. And yet she was seeking a way to cease being married to him.

Why?

Because she was terrified he would grow to loathe her, and that she couldn't bear.

For long moments, Mrs. Dove-Lyon remained silent. Her eyes glinted in the gloom. "Naïve woman. You haven't even given your marriage time to cure before you've decided it won't be what you need it to be in the future. A future which is ever-changing and not guaranteed."

"I cannot take the chance I'll grow closer to him or him to me. A break years from now would be too painful." Though, she didn't know how that was possible, for it felt as if there was a gaping hole in her chest. She did her best to tamp down her tears. "Will you help me or not?" If her request was a touch snappy, she couldn't help it. The last few weeks had been trying.

"What will I receive in exchange if I arrange this for you?"

It was something that had worried Adriana the past three nights. "My servitude? I will work in the Lyon's Den in whatever capacity you have. It is all I have to give."

The other woman snorted. "A life of prostitution."

At least it would allow her to forget Montague and everything that made him so dear. Adriana gave a curt nod. "I told you that I am quite serious. My husband seems to adore my body, so why wouldn't other men?" Her chin quivered and she nearly lost her composure. "I only want Pennington to be happy."

"Away from him." The other woman snorted. "I rather doubt the earl would be pleased once he discovers his wife is willing to service other men while beneath this roof."

"Once the divorce is granted, he'll have no right to make demands on my time."

"While that is true, you refuse to see what is right before your face. Pennington will never agree to a divorce. He loves you."

Was that true? Her breath stalled as her chest ached. "But he must agree to the divorce! It's vital to his future."

"No, *you* are vital to his future, which is why I matched you in the first place."

"He hasn't said that!" If he had, would it have made a difference? Adriana couldn't say.

"For a woman married twice, you are still quite a novice at this. Men aren't going to willingly reveal their thoughts and feelings. And especially not the earl, who has spent years stunted in this arena." Mrs. Dove-Lyon rose to her feet in a rustle of dark taffeta. "However, I shall take up your challenge merely for my own amusement, for I enjoy seeing people squirm, especially those who are not properly grateful for the gifts I give them." She grabbed a smart-looking hat, placed it upon her head, and then arranged a half-veil of black netting over the upper portion of her face. "However, if Pennington comes after you, I shall put other, more serious things into play as punishment."

That gave her pause. "Why would he? The earl doesn't love me or care beyond the surface." Yet, the look in his eyes when she'd told him she was setting him free earlier that evening would forever haunt her. A man who didn't care wouldn't have seemed so desolate, so shattered, would he?

"We shall see." The widow gestured to her. "Come. Let us remove to the ladies' gallery. I have a feeling this night will be quite spectacular. At least for me."

"Why?" She rose to her feet and followed the other woman from the room.

"Wagering on the main floor has been brisk regarding you and the earl since you wed."

Shock slammed into Adriana. "Why?" She sounded like the world's dullest parrot.

"Many men wish to see how long your union will last. They wagered on how quickly he would bed you. They are currently wagering on whether or not he'll take a new mistress." Mrs. Dove-Lyon shrugged as if she didn't care that the words were like sharp-headed barbs through Adriana's chest. "It goes to follow that they will now wager on who will marry you once that divorce is obtained."

"That's horrible. I am nobody."

"Well, you certainly will be now that you've washed your hands of your husband. A life of prostitution cannot compare to what Pennington will bestow upon you."

She ignored the barb… and the truth. "To know men are wagering on various aspects of my life is sickening." The heat of embarrassment burned through her cheeks. "I shouldn't have come. I should have merely left him and hid."

"Oh, we are well past regret now, Lady Pennington." Mrs. Dove-Lyon continued through the corridors at a brisk pace.

"All of this merely reinforces my belief all men are bounders." Why had she ever consented to marry again? It had been a poor choice on her part, and now her heart was breaking.

Yet, this pain was clearly of her own making, and she was just uttering excuses.

"Except Montague," the widow said in a soft voice. "He is raw and real and honest in his emotions, which is something others would be hard-pressed to give you. Thus, the reason for my gaming hell. To help men like him find love when they assume they—and society—believe they are beyond hope."

Adriana gasped. "You enjoy matchmaking."

"Of course. I adore the challenge of it, and it's more fulfilling than wagering, but I have never encountered someone who wishes one of my matches reversed. And that, my dear, doesn't sit well." She shot Adriana a sharp glance that sent tremors of fright down her spine. "Perhaps if he wishes it, his next match will be able to overcome the trauma you've created." There was nothing but irritation in the widow's voice. "That is, if he can recover from such a betrayal."

Oh, God, I really have betrayed him. The urge to cast up her accounts grew strong, but Adriana swallowed to keep retching at bay. She didn't want to think about Montague with another woman, but if he were to find happiness in his life, he needed to.

Once in the gallery, she couldn't bring herself to pass the time in a chair. Instead, she stood at the wall that ran around the perimeter of the gallery and overlooked the main gambling floor. Gentlemen milled about the area. The low buzz of conversation filled the air. All the tables were packed with men placing wagers on various card games.

When her gaze happened to land on one man in particular, she paused. "What is *he* doing here?" For it was none other than Mr. Richard Somerford, and his expression was quite intense.

Mrs. Dove-Lyon chuckled. "Most nights that he is here, Mr. Somerford tells everyone he intends to rescue you from the beastly clutches of Lord Pennington. Once he screws his courage to the sticking point, that is." Her lips twitched. "Perhaps I should have matched him with you."

"Yes, well, give a man enough alcohol and that's exactly what will happen." At this point, Adriana was rather tired of men. "Mr. Somerford provokes absolutely no reaction in me."

"But you tossed aside the man who provides just that. How bitter you've become, Lady Pennington." The widow's hand flexed on top of the railing. "It isn't my fault I matched you with the man you needed but you've rejected him without care or thought."

"For his own good!" Why couldn't anyone understand that?

She sniffed. "I rather think it's for your own convenience because you don't want to explore a love that isn't perfect or what you've made it into in your imagination, or what you believe you have read about in books. For that you have my pity."

Was that true? Would she only accept a skewed view of love that only she could see? And worse yet, was her decision considered selfish or sacrificial?

Does he love me despite being broken?

"You suffer from one picture of what you think a marriage *should* be, yet you should know that there are many different options, and not one of them is perfect for everyone. That is the glory of it, what makes it exciting."

Should she have given Montague the benefit of the doubt? The muscles in her belly knotted with anxiety. "I think, perhaps, I have changed my mind." It was a mistake to come here, especially now with Mrs. Dove-Lyon's change in attitude. She needed to find her husband, talk with him, say the words that were in her heart to him before it was too late. "I no longer wish for a divorce."

"I don't think so, Lady Pennington." The other woman's chuckle sent chills over her skin. "Once you've entered into a verbal agreement with me as the owner of this house, that word is your bond." She winked. "And the house always wins."

There wasn't an opportunity to respond, for one of the doors at the side of the gambling floor slammed open. Montague strode in, his greatcoat dripping from the rain, his top hat just as wet, and anger flashing in his eyes. "Bring me the owner of this establishment!" The command echoed through the suddenly hushed room. "I demand to see Mrs. Dove-Lyon!"

"Oh, my goodness." He was so full of life that Adriana's breath caught in her chest. A tingle of need went down her spine. "I always forget how magnificent he is when he's in a temper."

"And he has every right to be. I mean, when a man is told his wife is leaving him with as flimsy an excuse as you've given, a man worth his salt will come after her to argue the point." Mrs. Dove-Lyon's grin was quite predatory. "I hope he's brought his beastly side. He shall need it."

"But I—"

"It matters not, Lady Pennington." The widow waved a hand. "You have made your choice. I must now make a few arrangements."

Adriana laid a hand on the other woman's arm. "What will you do?" Suddenly, fear curled through her chest, for both her and him.

Mrs. Dove-Lyon's eyes sparkled behind the veil. "Make Pennington suffer, of course." She removed Adriana's hand. "Make him figure out what exactly he wants from his life, and in the process, show you that you made a poor choice by coming to me a second time with such an ungrateful attitude. I think, perhaps, you will lose this time around."

That sounded all too ominous. "But none of this is his fault. If you wish to punish someone, it should be me."

"Oh, I quite agree." Mrs. Dove-Lyon encircled her wrist with her strong fingers. "Come with me. This night should prove entertaining, and I cannot wait to see how it ends."

"But I don't want to—"

"Too late, my dear." The other woman fairly dragged Adriana around the wall toward a set of narrow stairs. "I wonder how far you will go to convince the angry earl you love him despite acting the coward?"

CHAPTER FIFTEEN

MONTAGUE HAD NEVER been as livid or as terrified as he was in this moment. If Adriana thought to leave him without more of an explanation than she'd given, she had another thing coming, and if Mrs. Dove-Lyon would aid and abet her, there *would* be hell to pay. At all costs, he would keep his wife with him, for she hadn't died. When death came calling, he hadn't a choice, but now he did.

She is mine, damn it all to hell, and I say when—or if—we are through.

Unfortunately, the first person he saw on the gambling floor was that man who'd been talking to Adriana the night she'd fled to Hyde Park. He was as good as any person in which to vent his spleen. "You, there!" Montague strode over the floor, weaving through the various tables until he reached the other man. "What the hell did you say to her?"

"I beg your pardon?" His red-gold hair gleamed nearly copper in the candlelight. "I haven't talked to anyone, let alone a woman, in recent days."

"Liar!" He stopped short of grabbing the man by his cravat. "I saw you talking with my wife one night in Hyde Park a couple of weeks ago. What did you tell her?" When a few raindrops dripped from the brim of his beaver felt top hat, Montague whipped it off and slapped it against his leg. "What nonsense did you say to her that made her leave me?"

More than a few gasps circulated through the room, and some of them were quite excited. No doubt there had been wagers thrown down on how long it would take until the union fell apart.

Bastards, all of them.

One of Somerford's eyebrows rose. "Adriana left you?"

Montague wished to punch the interest right off the man's face. "Not exactly, and I followed her here besides." This time, when he left the Lyon's Den, it would be with his wife and their marriage would be intact. Because he needed her. "I will *not* lose this fight."

"Ah, Lord Pennington," Mrs. Dove-Lyon said as she entered the gambling floor with Adriana in tow. Yet another veil covered the upper portion of her face. Why did the woman absolutely need to steep herself in mystery?

"Let us dispense with the pleasantries." He did not have the time to waste on such things. "I am here to convince my wife she doesn't need to go to such extremes." As he attempted to step around the proprietress of the establishment and reach Adriana, Mrs. Dove-Lyon moved to block his path.

"Ah, then you have reverted to your snapping, snarling ways." An enigmatic smile took possession of her lips that had been darkened with some sort of cosmetic. "I seem to recall you told my staff you would never again darken the doors of the Lyon's Den."

He shrugged, but the bulk of his attention was on his wife. Adriana stood, tensed as if to run, but she was still very much a vision in that saffron gown with the jewels sparkling at her throat and wrist. "Circumstances have changed."

"Then you lied when you said you had shaken the dust of this place from your boots."

"I meant it at the time." The words came out around a growl.

Truly, the woman didn't need to make this so difficult.

"Mmhmm." She made a show of glancing about the area before resting her gaze on him once more. Speculation and avarice sparkled in her eyes behind that veil. "Yet here you are. I can only wonder why."

He narrowed his gaze. "You know why." The longer he spoke with the Widow of Whitehall, the more a ring of onlookers gathered about them. Some of the men blatantly gawked at Adriana, and he hated each pair of eyes the fell upon his wife clad in that spectacular gown that showed her charms to advantage. "I would talk to Lady Pennington."

"That will prove a problem, Your Lordship." Again, she moved in front of Adriana, effectively blocking her from his view. "You see, she has engaged my services and wished to make use of my reach and power. Our verbal contract is quite binding."

The words slammed into his chest, battered his heart. "She intends to chase a divorce." It wasn't a question.

Another round of gasps and whispered snatches of conversation went around the room. Did the men make new wagers, or were they already assembling snippets of this latest scandal to circulate through society?

"Oh, yes. She does indeed, and what she has offered me in exchange is quite toothsome. To me, at least. After all, I *am* a businesswoman."

A muscle ticced in Montague's cheek. He wished he'd waited and brought Ashbury with him for moral support, but he hadn't been thinking that far ahead. "What is the offer?" Perhaps he could buy back whatever Adriana had given the widow.

"I'm quite certain the cost is too high, Your Lordship. Even for you."

"Tell me what the contract states," he demanded around clenched teeth. If the *beau monde*—as well as his own wife—assumed he was a beast and would never be anything else, perhaps he would live up to their expectations.

Reputation be damned.

Healing be damned.

The hush in the room was palpable. And the widow's grin widened. "Your wife has asked that I make arrangements and front the coin in order to procure a divorce. In exchange, she had agreed to become one of my courtesans." At the gasps from some of the men closest to the conversation, her eyes gleamed. "I'm sure Lady Pennington will be one of the more popular ladies once she's in service upstairs. Wouldn't you say, Your Lordship?"

"What the hell?" Montague's bottom jaw dropped. He stared at Adriana. "Do you hate me so much you are willing to sell your services multiple times a week to the highest bidder?" The pain surrounding his heart had reached unimaginable levels. He clasped a hand over that organ, for he feared it might attack him. "To let another man touch you so intimately?"

How the devil have I failed her?

"No, of course not!" Agony propelled the words out and reflected in her expression. "I am doing this *for* you, to set you free."

"Can you not see I have no wish for that?" He wanted to pull out his hair in frustration. "That I am inordinately happy with you?" What sort of maggot had got into her brain, that was clouding her thinking and skewing her judgment? To make her hide again?

"Ah, this will surely be the event of the month." Mrs. Dove-Lyon roved her gaze about at the crowd. "It seems the earl is most anxious to talk with his wife before their lives shift once again. However, since I make my living on funds collected through gambling, why not make a game out of it?" Her shrug was elegance and grace, as if she were in the Regent's drawing room instead of a gaming hell where she dictated the rules—both spoken and not—and she orchestrated the fate of every man beneath her roof. "After all, since apparently neither of you have taken your vows seriously, nor have you shown the proper appreciation for the match I put together, we shall treat your union as a game."

"That is hardly fair." He shot a glance at Adriana, and for a few seconds, their eyes connected. Pain, grief, and embarrassment reflected in those depths. "Do you truly wish for this?" If she couldn't stomach a lifetime with him, if she didn't return his regard, if she would never find a way to be happy as his wife, he would have no choice but to let her gain the freedom a divorce would bring.

And he would never again let himself fall in love.

Never.

He might as well be dead, for romance was as fatal as poison.

Before she could answer, Mrs. Dove-Lyon tsked her tongue. "Now, now, Lord Pennington. Don't cheat already. If you wish to converse with your countess, you'll have to play for that chance."

"What?" Surely, she didn't mean what he thought.

Mrs. Dove-Lyon nodded. When she snapped her fingers, one of the hulking male escorts shouldered his way through the crowd. "Just what I said." Then she addressed her employee. "Clear the closest table. The earl will make his last stand here." Once more, she eyed Montague. "This is one of the most important games you will play in your life. I hope your skill matches your boasting."

"You know it does. And if I don't wish to play?" He crossed his arms at his chest, regardless that he crushed his hat.

"I shall have you tossed out in the street, and life will go on without you. You won't even have the luxury of trying to fight for what you want." She pointed to the newly cleared table, but the crowds surrounding it had built even more. "Sit, Your Lordship."

He glowered. "Who am I playing against?" If that was what it took for him to leave with Adriana, so be it.

"Mr. Somerford, of course." Mrs. Dove-Lyon plucked the other man from the crowd and gave him a little shove toward the table. "He has been enamored with Lady Pennington before she became a countess, so it's only right that he play opposite you."

Bloody, *bloody* hell. Montague glared at the younger man as they both took chairs at the table. "What are the stakes?" What he really wished to do was throw over the table, knock down the chair, tear the curtains from the windows at this effrontery, but the threat of being physically separated from his wife held him back.

"Fifty thousand pounds to enter the game. It goes directly to the house coffers." When the widow cocked an eyebrow, both he and Mr. Somerford nodded, though the younger man blanched slightly.

"And the gain?"

She grinned as if she were most clever patroness in all of London. "If Pennington wins, he will receive the privilege of talking with his wife for a half hour." Her grin held a wicked edge. "If Mr. Somerford wins, that precious conversation is forfeit and *he* can have a conversation of his own with her."

"The devil you say!" Montague stood up from his chair so quickly that it toppled over, crashed against the highly polished wood floor.

"Or rather the devil I am, Your Lordship," Mrs. Dove-Lyon said with a decided smirk. She gestured to the crowd. One of the men righted the chair. The hulking escort laid a beefy hand on Montague's shoulder and forced him into it. "Faro is the card game I've selected. May the best man win."

"This is outside of enough," Montague groused as a deck of cards was procured by yet another of the workers from the Lyon's Den. "How dare you decide when or how I shall talk to my wife." He fairly shook from anger and exasperation as he threw his battered top hat to the floor.

"I can and I will, especially when the two of you cannot leave me out of the contretemps of your union because the pair of you are too blind to see."

"That you manipulated in the first place!"

"I inherently know things that you do not." Frost had formed in the widow's voice as she stared him down. "And if you choose to now waste my time, then I shall do what I please with that time." She waved a hand. "Take Lady Pennington to a private gaming room. Under no circumstances is she allowed to leave."

When another large male escort arrived on the scene, Montague moved to vacate his chair again, but the hulking guard kept him steady. "Do not think to lay a hand on her."

"Pennington!" Adriana's alarmed cry pierced right through his chest. "Don't let them take me away! I never meant for any of this to happen."

At least there was that. Though the admission had come too late.

Mrs. Dove-Lyon snorted with apparent enjoyment. "You may engage in fisticuffs later, Lord Pennington, but just now, you have more important things to attend." She rested her gaze on his opponent. "Whenever you are ready, Mr. Somerford. You shall be the dealer since you are more trustworthy than His Lordship."

A plague on all the women currently in my life.

When it appeared there was no stopping the game as Mr. Somerford dealt out the cards, Montague settled into his chair and hunched his shoulders. He believed in his skill at the table and knew he could rout this pup in short order, but would talking to Adriana do any good? And why the devil did she assume he even wished to be set free from their union?

Card after card flipped. Wager after wager was made. Montague lost some. Somerford won some. Then their luck reversed, and still round after round went onward. Chips were exchanged back and forth. His talent for card games was superior to his opponent, but Somerford was scrappy, and he desperately wanted what Montague already had—access to Adriana.

Side wagers went up among the crowd that had formed around their table. Calls of encouragement circulated; some for him and some for Somerford.

Finally, it all came down to the last two cards. The one flipped was the Queen of Hearts. Ironic, that, but Montague didn't care. "I wager the other card will be higher in rank than this one." Gasps went through the crowd, for it was a bold move, but he *had* been paying attention. He arched an eyebrow. There were only two cards it could possibly be—the Two of Spades and the King of Hearts. Most of his good fortune at the tables was counting cards and learning how to hold his liquor so his mind remained sharp. "What say you, Somerford?"

The younger man wiped at the perspiration on his upper lip. "I rather doubt there is anything of value left in the deck that will win against the queen."

Mrs. Dove-Lyon grinned. "Final wagers."

Montague shoved all of his chips to the center. "That is my final wager." Those chips represented near seventy-five thousand pounds. He didn't much care about the coin; he merely wanted his wife.

Mr. Somerford appeared a bit green about the edges of his mouth. No doubt if he lost the hand, he would be near dun territory. "I stand by my decision."

The onlookers leaned forward as a hush went through the room. Slowly, ever so slowly, Mr. Somerford flipped over the final card.

Montague shuddered with relief to see the King of Hearts staring back at him. Another bit of irony, for the hearts were the suit of love, and the king was nothing without his queen. Just as he had likened his life without Adriana in it. As victory surged through him, Montague stood. He rested his narrowed gaze on Mrs. Dove-Lyon as he rose to his feet. "Take me to my wife."

"Very well." She snapped her fingers. The burly man who'd guarded the table jerked his massive head. Seconds later, he'd cleared a path through the crowds, and Montague followed him through the warren of corridors until they reached one of the private wagering rooms. Mrs. Dove-Lyon had come along too. "You have thirty minutes, then you will need to play the remaining game."

He didn't deign to comment, but when he attempted to close the door behind him, his guard shook his head. "What rubbish is this?"

The owner of the Lyon's Den shrugged. "I never said it would be a *private* conversation, and you are too cunning besides. I don't want you to abscond with my investment prematurely."

Damn and blast.

The woman was a trial, but he nodded and then promptly forgot her in favor of looking at Adriana, who sat on one of the chairs at the round card table. A crystal glass with a measure of brandy waited beside a bottle, but it didn't appear that either had been touched.

As he approached the table, the silvery tracks of tears on her cheeks betrayed the fact she'd been crying, but he hardened his heart as a way to further protect that already shattered organ. "Why did you come here instead of talking to me?" he asked as he dropped into the only other chair at the table.

"Because you would have tried to charm me with words and kiss-es, and when that happens, confusion takes hold of my mind, distracting me from my purpose." She looked at him, and there was such sorrow and confliction in the brown depths of her eyes, that his chest tightened. "I meant what I said, Montague," she continued a low voice with a glance at Mrs. Dove-Lyon who stood just outside the room.

"Even though you wished to call a halt to the preceding just now?"

"I..."

Best get on with it and to the heart of the matter. Perhaps she'd fallen into old habits and ways of thinking that no longer served her. "You mean to set me free." It wasn't a question. When she nodded, he huffed in annoyance. "I don't want my freedom."

"But if you don't take it now, this marriage will become your pris-on eventually." Adriana scrubbed at the tears on her cheeks. "You want children; I have seen that truth in your eyes more than a few times." When he went to deny that claim, she held up a hand. "Your duty to your title demands that you produce an heir. We both know this. It is your destiny." The muscles in her throat worked with a hard swallow. "I cannot give you a child, Montague; thus, the reason I am setting you free."

"Yes, yes, you've told me all of this before."

"Then why aren't you listening?" Her voice rose with each word. "You never listen, which makes you just like everyone else in my life." Anger flashed in her eyes. Twin spots of color blazed on her pale cheeks. "You have no need for a wife who cannot give you everything you need."

Her anger prodded his own, and he'd been under too much emotional stress these past few days to deny that outlet. "You never once asked me what *I* wanted from a wife!" It was a truth even she couldn't deny. "Since day one of this marriage, everyone else assumed they knew what was best for me, what I wanted from a union, how I should act therein."

Surprise jumped into her eyes. "You are quite correct. Never once did it occur to me to ask that question, for I have been too consumed with various other issues." She clasped her hands together on the tabletop. "What *do* you want from marriage?"

He didn't miss the fact that she didn't say "our marriage" and that worked to further irritate him. "I want…" What? Never had he examined the yearnings of his soul before, for grief and anger had swept him away, stuffed him into a desolate place where hope didn't reside. "I want to make a difference in someone's life," he admitted in a soft voice as he looked at his wife. "To leave my mark and my legacy."

"While I won't deny that you have certainly made a difference in my life—in so many ways—it would be difficult for you to have a legacy with no children." She reached out a hand, briefly touched one of his before retreating. "Don't you see that?"

"No one ever said a legacy was tied up in having children." Why was this a sticking point on her agenda? "I have several charities I champion. Perhaps one of those will prove popular soon." Then another thought occurred to him. "But I am also a painter of small acclaim. That is indeed legacy worthy."

And damn if he didn't wish to paint Adriana as she was now—a dab of summer fading into autumn in that gown, with her brown eyes luminous, and her lips parted as if she were anticipating a kiss. His shaft stirred. What was stopping him from spiriting her away from this place and then having his wicked way with her in the carriage?

A glance to the door where Mrs. Dove-Lyon stood with the hulking escort answered his question. They were much like prisoners here, but why? What did the widow want from them?

When Adriana didn't respond, he rushed to continue. "I want to be remembered for something other than being the worst man in London, and…" The words stalled, for this next admission would render him weak in her eyes. "I thought I had that on the day I gave you the use of my library," he said in a low voice. "I had hoped we'd reached a turning point in our relationship that day. But if not at that time, then surely when I shared my history with you, when you saw me at my lowest point, and you accepted me anyway." His voice broke. "Can you not see me for something other than a beast? See yourself for something other than less?"

"Oh, Montague." She touched his hand again, and this time he clasped it, vowing to himself not to let her get away. "You are, of course you are a man to be proud of, and you are no longer the beast I married."

"Because of your guidance, your acceptance." Why couldn't she see that he needed her, and that she needed him? "Your love." It was bold of him to announce it, but would she deny it?

Yet, she'd never said anything like that to him. Was she too headstrong for that? Did she truly not need him? Not care for him?

He waited with held breath.

"No, because of *your* will and want to change. It was always there. I merely provoked it out of you." Her smile held a sad tinge. "I fear, though, if we remain wed and you continue to find my shortcomings that you will grow to hate me."

"Everyone has flaws, sweeting. No one is perfect, and thank God for that. Perfection is cold with no room to grow."

She snorted. "I wanted that after my last marriage, and when it became all too evident you were indeed nowhere near perfection, I…"

Now he understood at least a bit of the puzzle she presented. "You were disappointed and convinced our union would end like the last one because of your warped ideal of what a union should be." Some of the weight on his shoulders lessened. "The inability to bear children is merely the crutch you lean on, the wedge you are using to drive us apart. An excuse."

"No!" Adriana shook her head so vehemently that a lock of hair tumbled to her shoulder. "That is a valid concern. What if we remained married and you are everything lovely, but your acceptance of me starts to feel like pity? Will I resent you because of it?"

"Only you can say if that is true or not." But he hoped she didn't. None of this was bringing them closer. "The one other thing I always hoped to have after the deaths of my fiancées was love." It was another truth he'd kept to himself. "I long for love and to be loved in return, though I wonder now if I've ruined my chance."

Adriana slammed a hand onto the table so hard the glass clinked against the bottle. "You have to be willing to give away that emotion before it can come back to you, Pennington!" Once more, high color decorated her cheeks. "Why the devil would any woman in her right mind wish to remain wed to you if love isn't present? A wonderful library and lovely intercourse aside, none of those things matter if we don't have love."

For the second time that night, his jaw dropped. Was that the crux of contention, then? That they hadn't exchanged words of love? That they were both still hiding behind fears to avoid uttering those few precious words so they wouldn't be hurt or rejected? And neither of them wished to be the first to admit it due to past experience?

Well, we are a fine pair, then.

"I—"

Mrs. Dove-Lyon swept into the room. "Your time is up, Lord Pennington."

"Poppycock! We have only begun."

Her grin was victorious. "You knew the rules."

As the burly escort came back into the room, he brought Mr. Somerford with him. Montague glared. "I demand another game." Men poured into the room with the intent to watch.

"Of course, Your Lordship. Only this time, you will play against your countess." When he and Adriana stared at her, she continued. "The stakes are much higher now, since we're coming to the potential end of this union, and nothing was worked out during that talk."

Anger pummeled Montague's insides. "We need more time."

"Too bad." Mrs. Dove-Lyon shook her head. "You didn't make good use of what I allowed. So, if Pennington wins, he will remain married to the lovely Adriana, but she will spend the rest of her viable years working for me here at the Lyon's Den as a courtesan."

Shock delivered a punch to his gut. "What sort of deviltry is this? I will not allow my wife to be abused."

Adriana shook her head as horror clouded her eyes. "That wasn't the deal."

Mrs. Dove-Lyon ignored them both. "If the countess wins, she'll have her freedom from our verbal contract *and* your union, but will then immediately marry Mr. Somerford by way of contracts and a license, both of which I shall procure before dawn." Her smile positively dripped manipulation. "After all, there is no sort of future for a lady with a battered reputation and trailing scandal. She might as well be wed to someone."

Murmurs went through the crowd. Mr. Somerford seemed genuinely surprised. Had he been caught up in this vortex as an innocent bystander, or had this been his game all along?

"Bah." Montague glared at the widow. "This is untenable."

Mrs. Dove-Lyon shrugged. "You brought this on yourself from failure to communicate." She glanced at Adriana, who had paled and pressed gloved fingers to her lips, then she snapped her attention back to him. "What do you want more, Lord Pennington? The heart of the woman but not her body? What do *you* want, Lady Pennington? To have the perfect marriage to a noble man, but not engage your own heart despite the difficulties?"

Damn, damn, damn.

CHAPTER SIXTEEN

ADRIANA WANTED NOTHING more than to perhaps cast up her accounts and then hide herself away from the multiple pairs of prying or lascivious eyes. The fact the owner of the Lyon's Den had used both her words and Montague's against them had bile sailing up the back of her throat.

Mrs. Dove-Lyon had taken her deal and had warped it into something heinous and horrifying. Though she might not have wanted to marry Pennington initially, they had both weathered the storm enough that they could build a foundation upon the ground revealed, and she certainly didn't wish to marry Mr. Somerford.

How the devil had he come to be caught up in this particular scandal?

She glanced at him. "Please tell her you do not want this."

"I think perhaps I do." He snorted in apparent amusement. "If I can take you away from Lord Pennington, which had been my hope all along, it was good, but now that I can have you as *my* wife, it's even better."

Oh, she had had her fill of men! "Yet, there again, no one bothered to ask me what *I* want."

"Except, you already told me, Your Ladyship," Mrs. Dove-Lyon inserted with a grin that was far from genuine. "You wished to be rid of your husband. No matter how the game goes, you shall have that."

Tears sprang into her eyes. She looked at Montague, saw the anguish in his expression, and a cry escaped. "I don't want it like this." Either choice was a travesty.

"Then you should have been grateful for the match I arranged initially."

"Ha!" Adriana shook her head. "Thanks to *me*. If I hadn't taken my sister's place, I wouldn't have married Pennington at all."

"Indeed, that is the truth, but if I hadn't helped make that come to pass, neither of you would be sitting here now. The earl would have married dear Sybil and would have probably already gotten her with child." Mrs. Dove-Lyon shrugged. "Yet I saved him from marrying a woman too young and immature. Where is my thanks for that?"

"I don't want Mr. Somerford."

That man bristled. "I can give you everything he can't—or won't."

Except love. Would you give me that? Would Montague have declared his feelings had they not been interrupted? This whole night was maddening.

"Seems to me you don't want Lord Pennington either. Many women would jump at the chances you have been presented." The widow glanced between them. "I think the earl shall be the dealer for this game of faro, for it's rather unlikely the countess has had much experience in this realm." She winked at Adriana. "I do hope the odds are in your favor, my dear, for I won't take an interest in your future a third time."

A deck of cards was brought to the table as well as chips for wagering. All the while, Montague watched her as if she had betrayed him in the worst way possible.

Perhaps she had. In trying to tell him she wasn't good enough for him, she'd inadvertently shown that she thought *he* wasn't enough for *her.* She had taken their beautiful time together and ground it beneath her heel, even if she didn't feel that way.

How can I fix this?

Her hands trembled as Montague dealt the cards and arranged a row of them along the side of the table. Of the two in the middle, he flipped one over. A six of spades. The other he left alone for the time being. As he glanced at her, his mouth was set into a hard line. Though he'd taught her how to play faro, she wasn't a good guesser and she had never quite understood the trick of counting or watching the cards as they were played like he did.

Every move, every decision she would make from this point forward would determine how she would spend her future.

And she hated every moment of it. *Why couldn't I have left well enough alone?*

"No time like the present, Lady Pennington," Mrs. Dove-Lyon prompted.

"Fine." She tossed a few chips into the center of the table. "I'll wager the new card is higher."

Montague placed a bet of his own, only he said the card would be lower. Then he flipped the second card. The ten of diamonds. "The lady wins."

Several rounds followed, and with every wager, he took the opposite stance of hers. All too soon, a pattern emerged.

"You are throwing your bets." Adriana frowned. Did he not care about the outcome of this game?

"No, I am giving you what you want—freedom." He added a few chips to the growing pile.

"That's *not* what I want!" she hissed and glared at him through narrowed eyes.

"Frankly, Countess, I'm not certain you know what you want at all." He lifted a dark eyebrow, daring her to contradict him. "I have tried to give you everything, but you resisted me at every turn."

"I certainly don't want to become a courtesan, even if it means staying married to you." She tamped on the urge to cry. How had they landed in this mess?

"That is good to know, but I don't want Somerford to have you either."

The man scoffed. "You are not good enough for her."

"Oh, don't I know it?" Montague's expression turned sad. "She deserves so much more than what I am."

Did that mean he loved her enough to forgive everything? Perhaps it was time to put everything on the proverbial table—her heart, her hopes, her fears, her dreams, all of it. Wager it all. "Please don't devalue yourself. You are enough, but I want you to be happy. It's all I have ever wanted since day one."

"Ha." He snorted. "If that were so, you wouldn't have sought out a divorce from the devil's own minion over there." With a slight lift of his chin, he indicated Mrs. Dove-Lyon.

"But giving you a child will make you happy. Since I cannot do that, I want you to marry someone who can." *Because I love you.*

"Are you even listening to yourself?" Though he kept his voice low, there was no mistaking the annoyance in those tones. "You complained that no one asked you what you wanted from life or a marriage, yet you are doing the same to me. It's deuced aggravating." When his eyes met hers, such sorrow was reflected there that it tugged at her heart. "I don't need children to make my life complete, Adriana. I don't want someone else as my wife, and I certainly refuse to let you leave me for someone else." His voice broke. "I want *you*. Need *you*. Come what may, I shall *only* want you."

Was he only saying that to play to her empathy? "Why, to keep your beastly side at bay?" She frowned at the cards on the table. Whose turn was it?

"Of course not." His fingers clenched and unclenched upon the tabletop. "I only had to make the conscious decision to let go of that anger to transform. Though it's a constant decision, I did that for you."

"You should have done it for yourself." If she sounded more wasp-ish than she liked, it couldn't be helped. This whole evening had become impossible.

"But none of it would have come about if it weren't for *you*." He pointed at the card. "The first one will be higher."

Murmurs went through the crowd, and she despised every single person present.

"What a jackanapes you are, Pennington." She rolled her eyes. "The second card is the higher of the pair." Of course, when she turned the card over, her prediction was true. Shards of anger went through her chest, for she would *not* marry Mr. Somerford. "Why are you doing this?"

"Since you apparently could never be happy with me unless we have children, I am giving you what you want—a life with Mr. Somerford. He is everything I am not. Perfect. Wasn't that what you wanted?"

"No!" She shoved all the chips she'd won back at him. "I don't want him. I don't want perfection. I don't want anything except you!"

"Yet here we are. *You* made this decision."

"Under duress! My life has changed, shifted, in so many ways since I met you, that I wished to make you as happy as you have made me."

"By calling for a divorce? By leaving? The scandal alone will bury us both, and how the hell can we be happy then?"

"As if scandal hasn't already buried us?" Would they be shunned from the *ton* now?

"Bah. I care nothing for all of that. I care only that being married, finding you, has made my life worthwhile after so much struggle." A muscle in his cheek ticced, and when he held her gaze, his roiled with so much sadness and anger that it broke her heart. She'd done this to him. "I lost my fiancées to death, Adriana. That wasn't something I could fight, but I will be damned if I let you slip away from me over something as insignificant as you thinking you aren't worthy due to your reproduction status or anything else those deuced fears tell you."

Tears misted her eyes. "I want you to be happy, Montague."

"I will be if you'd just see what's in front of your eyes!" He thumped a fist onto the table. The glass of brandy slipped perilously close to the edge. "You are exactly the sort of woman I need in my life."

She snorted. "I'm not your usual type."

"In that, I was wrong, and have since changed my mind." He didn't give quarter. "I want you even when you're acting as maddening as you are now."

"As if you aren't behaving like an arse?" Adriana tossed a chip at him. "I want a life where I won't need to struggle or avoid a man's fists."

"You can have both of those things with me. Aside from those first days of our marriage, I have treated you with nothing except respect and care."

Of course he would say that. "I'd venture to say there was rather only desire and lust those first days." Saying it aloud put heat in her cheeks.

"Truth." An answering flush crept over his collar. "Not that it has faded."

Adriana refused to stroke his ego… or anything else just now lest she become distracted again. "I want someone to be proud of me."

"Shouldn't you be proud of yourself and everything you have already accomplished—already survived?" he responded in a fair parrot of what she'd told her a few minutes ago. When she narrowed her eyes, he gave her a tight grin. "I have never ceased being amazed by you let alone proud. Hell, sweeting, I wanted to shout my good fortune from the rooftop tonight when we were at the ball, so that everyone would know how much I adore you."

Oh, dear God. Tingles went down her spine while flutters danced through her belly. "You did?"

"Yes." He eyed the bottle of brandy but didn't reach for it. "But then you broke my heart and fled here thinking to tear me away from you, as if *I* don't matter."

"You do, though."

"Ha." His gaze strayed to Mrs. Dove-Lyon, who watched their interaction with intense interest. "In moments, I will lose you forever in the worst way possible to that bastard." He flicked his gaze to Mr. Somerford.

"I hardly think that's a bad thing, Your Lordship," the man shot off. "I will treat her like a queen. She will never need to lift a finger."

"No doubt you will, but I rather suspect Adriana wouldn't enjoy being pampered for the rest of her life. She is too talented in arguing, and I suspect she has a wicked right hook if provoked enough." When his chin trembled, that tell of vulnerability sliced straight through to her soul. He glanced back at her. "So if this is the last conversation you and I enjoy, I have nothing left to lose."

Mrs. Dove-Lyon tsked. "Play the cards, Pennington."

The earl ignored her. "We haven't been married very long, but I want the opportunity to show you our union wasn't a mistake, to show you there will never come a day when I don't look forward to seeing you, talking with you, arguing with you... bedding you."

Snickers and whispers went through the crowd.

Oh, he was so sweet when he opened himself up for potential ridicule or rejection. Her cheeks heated. Perhaps she should do the same and be honest with him, for she wouldn't have another chance. "I want a marriage that will last."

"Then give ours a chance." His fingers paused over his chips.

Am I strong enough? "I want a union that will never grow stale."

A trace of amusement flared in his eyes. "I don't imagine ours will if the heat between us is any indication." He lowered his voice. "I haven't had you nearly enough in my bed."

"Or in your carriage?" she asked in a barely audible whisper.

"Or against a wall," he murmured.

"Or on the floor?" How could she have thought to leave him?

Murmurs and winks were bandied about the onlookers, while Mr. Somerford's face turned red in either embarrassment or anger.

"I don't want a perfect marriage as Mrs. Dove-Lyon indicated." Her hand shook on the tabletop. "I rather like how messy ours has been. It is easier to judge growth."

"It provides a lovely challenge," he added, and some of the shadows left his eyes. "As do you, and that only endears you to me more."

Tears sprang to her eyes. "But you should know, I don't want you."

"What?" His eyes rounded in shock.

Gasps echoed through the hush of the room.

Heat slapped at her cheeks. "Want is a very temporary thing, Pennington. It changes all too often. To that end, while I might *want* you in the moment, I *need* you for the rest of my life." Her throat went dry, but this needed to be said. It was the greatest gamble of her life. "Because... because..." She pressed her lips together, but there was nothing for it. "I love you. Not for your title, not for the power you wield, not because you are a little bit broken like I am, and certainly not for that secret persona you told me about, though that is *very* exciting to me."

A flush rose up his neck. His mouth worked but no sound came out.

Mrs. Dove-Lyon bustled over to the table. "The game is not over yet, and do remember, these stakes are high for a reason."

Adriana glanced at her and then at her husband, this man who had been through so much, who had had his heart broken three times— once by her—and she smiled. Nothing else mattered. There was a certain freedom in letting everything go and admitting to love.

"To be honest, Mrs. Dove-Lyon, your wagers and your rules can go hang." She shoved everything from the tabletop—cards, chips, brandy bottle and glass—and laughed when the crystal broke when it hit the floor. Then she stood, leaned over that piece of furniture, and grabbed Montague's cravat. "I love you, Montague Bassage. Only you, because of your courage and your vulnerability, your strength and your character. And if you were truthful about not having children, my love for you will only grow and expand."

"Damn, but you are quite the scandalous baggage," he whispered as he pushed to his feet. "Yes, I was telling the truth. I love you for that and for everything else you are. You are the puzzle I will quite happily spend the remainder of my life trying to solve." His gaze dropped briefly to her lips before he stared directly into her eyes. "I love you now and will do the same forever if you forget about this ridiculous notion of divorcing me."

"Of course." She was halfway across the table in a no-doubt scandalous position, but she didn't care. "Will you remain married to me?"

It was as if the sun had come out on a cloudy day when he smiled and the delicate skin at the corners of his eyes crinkled. "I will. With you, I no longer have cause to be the worst man in London." Then she was somehow in his arms, her arse sitting firmly on the tabletop, her legs dangling down and naturally parted, and him standing between her thighs as he kissed her with such determination and authority that she couldn't quite think of anything else in that moment.

Wild cheering and catcalls echoed through the room before it erupted into excited chatter and demands for champagne.

Adriana clung to her husband's large frame and unashamedly kissed him back until a hand on her shoulder wrenched them apart and she stared into the very angry face of Mr. Somerford. "Release me at once."

A growl issued from Montague, and then before Mr. Somerford could defend himself, the earl landed him a facer that sent the other man sprawling. "Do not think to lay a hand on her again."

Mr. Somerford regained his composure. He tugged on the hem of his jacket. "I cry foul. There was an agreement between me and Mrs. Dove-Lyon. I was to take Lady Pennington to wife. To save her."

The veiled owner of the gaming hell sauntered into view. "Take heart, Mr. Somerford, in the fact that you discovered how fickle Adriana clearly is. You wouldn't wish to wed a woman who loves another, would you? She would be rather a trial for you."

"But I—"

Mrs. Dove-Lyon snapped her fingers and the hulking escort appeared at Mr. Somerford's side. "I'm quite certain I can make other arrangements for your future." Once he was escorted from the room and many of the onlookers followed, she looked at Adriana. "I am glad you came to your senses. This whole charade of the wagers was, after all, an effort for you both to declare how you really felt for each other once fear had been shoved aside."

"I don't understand." She burrowed into Montague's side when he wrapped an arm around her waist.

Oddly enough, her husband chuckled. "In Mrs. Dove-Lyon's demented, manipulative brain, she wished to make certain her handiwork in matching us had taken correctly." The low rumble of his voice sent shivers of awareness down Adriana's spine. "She assumed that when the stakes were raised exponentially and we were both faced with scenarios we didn't want, we would stop hiding or making excuses—"

"—and declare yourselves." The widow smiled, but it was still as wicked as it had ever been. "Everyone in London assumes women cannot be clever and cunning, that we cannot wield power on our own and make people dance at our bidding." She shrugged. "And when one dangles the hope of love before stubborn men and recalcitrant women, I simply let fate and human nature do the rest."

"For a price, of course," Montague added in a soft voice.

"Of course. I am not running a charity, Lord Pennington." She bounced her bright gaze between them. "May you have many happy years ahead and may you both find everything you have ever dreamed in each other."

Adriana glanced up into her husband's face. "I have no doubts we will." Then she looked at the other woman. "Thank you for knowing what we did not."

"It was truly my pleasure." She waved them off. "Go. The night is young. If you both aren't in some form of undress in the next twenty minutes, I shall be disappointed."

"Come." Montague took Adriana's hand and tugged her toward the door. "Let us leave before she puts us through another gauntlet."

"I have no wish to be anywhere you are not." It felt as if her feet never touched the floor as he led her through the warren of corridors. For the first time in far too many years, she was content and happy and wrapped in such a warm blanket of love that she couldn't wait to live every day to its fullest.

And it was all due to a trip into the Lyon's Den.

Two, really.

"I couldn't be more pleased with my very own lion," she whispered.

Montague brought her to a halt in an empty hall. He pulled her into his arms and with a finger beneath her chin, tilted her head up until their gazes connected in the dimness. "Just wait until our life together unfolds. The adventure is only beginning."

Then he set out to apparently kiss her senseless.

EPILOGUE

December 23, 1821
Bassage House
London, England

"MONTAGUE? WILL YOU come in here please?"

He tilted his head at the sound of his wife's voice. Currently, he read a copy of *The Times* in his study, for that evening had been the only time he'd had to relax. Christmas was in two days, and he'd been constantly busy with finishing a handful of commissions for portraits ahead of the holiday season. Ever since he'd made the decision to go public with the name he painted under, that hobby had turned into an extremely profitable business that brought him joy.

However, he no longer painted scandalous portraits. The only woman he now portrayed nude on a canvas had been his wife.

"I'll be right there." With a last lingering glance at the article he'd started, he tossed aside the paper and then left the study. At the opposite end of the corridor, he came into the library where Adriana always retreated to when life became too busy, and she needed quiet.

For a few seconds, he stood at the door merely to peer at her in secret. Even though they'd passed their fourth anniversary not two months before, her unassuming beauty always caught him by surprise, and tonight was no exception.

Clad in a gown of red velvet—for they were due to attend a dinner at Ashbury's home in ninety minutes—she was every bit the Christmas season personified. Satan slept all stretched out at her side, and occasionally she would stroke a hand along his exposed belly.

She was the only one who could get away with that.

A bit of holly was pinned into her upswept blonde hair. Rubies glittered at her neck, wrist, and lobes. The parure had been an anniversary gift from him this year, and it suited her wonderfully well. But what continued to steal his breath whenever he painted her or when she dressed for a society event was the faint blush on her round cheeks and the sparkle of contentment in her rich brown eyes.

How had he ever thought, once upon a time, that she wasn't in his usual style?

Then she turned her head and glanced at him from over her shoulder with such an elf-like expression that he couldn't help but chuckle. "Why are you spying on me?"

"I would never do that." Montague came further into the room as she stood up from her spot in a chair near the fire. Never would he admit to watching her ever so often. "I was simply admiring you. Can a man not do that regarding the woman he loves?"

"You can, of course." She crossed the carpet and held out her hands to him. Unreadable emotion clouded her eyes. "There is something I must tell you, but you have to promise me that you will remain calm."

Immediately, his stomach dropped. "Are you well?" They had been at his estate in Essex for the past three months for a holiday of sorts to celebrate their anniversary, and on the way home, she'd been nauseous a few times but said it was nothing to worry about.

"Yes. I believe so." Happiness danced in her eyes, yet it was different than what was usually there. Happiness and… shock. Joy, even. "Do you believe in miracles, Montague?" she asked in a soft voice.

"I never had cause to think about such things, for the last miracle I had in my life was you." They weren't words for romance; they were merely the truth.

"Aww." She squeezed his fingers, drew him over to the sofa. When Adriana sat, she pulled him down beside her. "A few days ago, I had a physician in since I still felt queasy from our holiday."

Please God let her be well. Remembering the drawn-out agony of his second fiancée's sickness loped through his mind. He wasn't strong enough to survive that again. "And?" His throat was so tight he could barely speak.

"I hadn't put much thought into the signs or symptoms because we just assumed… I mean to say I wasn't thinking along those lines…"

"Adriana." He clung to her hands. "Please, for the love of God, tell me what the diagnosis was." If she was ailing, he would do whatever he could to save her. Death wouldn't win this time around.

If her eyes held any more stars, he would swear she'd swallowed a portion of the heavens. "I am increasing. Three months along, which would explain why some of my gowns are suddenly too tight. I knew I hadn't eaten more sweets than normal."

"I don't… Are you certain…? How is that possible?" He stared at her as if he'd never seen her before. "You are… pregnant?" No matter how he tried, he simply couldn't wrap his head around the news.

"Yes." She nodded, and then her eyes were luminous with unshed tears. "I had long ago given up on that dream. It wasn't a vital part of our marriage. We had both made our peace regarding never having children, and we have been quite happy just the two of us." A shrug lifted her shoulder and pulled her bodice tighter over her bosom. "Yet here we are."

"I am stunned." Hell, he couldn't understand how such a thing had happened after so many years of not having been successful. "Are you happy?"

"Wonderfully so." She put a hand against the side of his face. "But please know I am extraordinarily happy with you. With us. This is only glitter on an already fantastic life. My feelings for you won't change."

"Good." He nodded though his chest was still tight from the shock of the announcement. "So, an infant in June, then?"

"Yes." A giggle escaped her. "Are you pleased?"

"I am stunned, but once I have a chance to think properly upon the notion, I will be over the moon with joy." It had finally happened. He would be a father, and he might have an heir after all. He took her hand and pressed a kiss into her palm. "A child. After so long." After the doctor had told them years ago that there was nothing clinically wrong with Adriana's body but that the female form remained much a mystery. "Our child."

Truly, it was the best gift he could have received for Christmas.

"I can scarcely let myself hope just yet in the event that something happens."

"It is good to be cautious, but sweeting, do you realize how surprising this is? How completely wonderful?" Not knowing how to act, he caught her head between his palms and then claimed her lips in a long, lingering series of kisses. And like every time he sent time kissing his wife, need turned his blood to fire and tightened his shaft. "I love you so much."

The way she looked at him made him feel as if he could do anything as well as want to ravish her right there. "I love you too, but the doctor said my advanced age could prove a hinderance."

"Pish posh, my dear. You are *not* old." But it was a valid concern. "I will watch you like a hawk, and will pamper you until the birth."

"I'm not an invalid."

"No, but you are more precious to me than everything else, and I won't take any chances that something could harm you." He kissed her again, and when the longcase clock in the corridor beyond chimed the seven o'clock hour, he pulled slightly away. "We are due at Ashbury's in an hour, but—"

Adriana giggled. "I think we have enough time for a bit of fun before we must leave for his home." She slipped a hand up his chest to curl about his nape. "Unless you don't wish to out of fear it might damage me or the babe."

"Now I know that is wildly untrue." He eased her backward on the sofa, much to the annoyance of the cat.

Satan uttered a few choice meows and then removed himself from their presence.

"How do you know?"

"Remember, darling, I was the worst man in London before I married you." Montague didn't wish to talk about that time in his life, for it was firmly in his past. This woman, the wonderful woman who carried their babe in her belly, was his present and his future. With that, he couldn't be happier.

"Hmm, I shall need to do a better job of banishing those women from your mind." She squealed when he manipulated her gown enough to ease her bodice down.

"I was an idiot to overlook your charms in the beginning, when I thought I wanted willowy thin women instead of a painter's dream." He kissed first one breast and then the other. Those taut pink tips never failed to stoke his arousal. "You have completely managed to upend my life and make it into something to be proud of."

Never did he think it was possible, but she had managed to prove him wrong too many times to not believe she was the change he'd needed.

"We did that together, Pennington. Don't forget it." With a sigh, she twined her arms about his shoulders and furrowed the fingers of one hand into his hair. "You know how I like it, especially when we're pressed for time."

"Hot, hard, and quick?" How he adored teasing her.

"Of course." That look in her eye held wicked promise. "Besides, I have been in great need of you for more than a few days."

Desire shot down his spine. "All right, but don't blame me if your gown is crushed by the time we arrive at Ashbury's dinner." Then he was lost in the wonders of his wife's body.

He took one of her nipples into his mouth, alternately sucking and soothing with his tongue while he bedeviled the other pebbled bud with his fingers. Always responsive, Adriana squirmed beneath him, and soon her soft cries and moans of pleasure filled the air. When she guided his lips to hers and she kissed him with the fervor to which he'd become accustomed, his hold on control slipped. His hands went beneath her skirting, and he skimmed her satiny skin.

In the summer, he would have a child. It was still too new, too overwhelming, that he couldn't quite believe it, but when he smoothed a palm over the rounded swell of her belly, he paused as awe fell over him. Oh, this child would be so loved! That little miracle, that unexpected surprise they had never expected, was growing even now inside his wife's body. The enormity of it staggered him, and quick tears stung the backs of his eyelids.

"Are you well, Pennington?"

"Oh, yes. Quite." In fact, he'd never been better. Pushing his thoughts to the back of his mind—for there was plenty of time to attend to them—he busied himself with thoroughly kissing his wife, and as he delved a hand between her splayed thighs and she wriggled with anticipation, he grinned against her lips. Over the past four years, they'd had much fun together.

Everything would only grow sweeter.

"Montague!"

"Hmm?" He'd barely strummed his fingers along her folds, but perhaps the pregnancy made her more sensitive to touch.

"Send me flying." She touched a hand to his, guiding him to where she needed him to be. "Hurry!"

"Always." Soon enough, he encouraged that swollen bud at her center out of hiding. Over and over, he stroked his fingers along it in varying degrees of friction, and he didn't stop.

Her breathing grew shallow and labored. She dug her fingernails into his shoulders while her back arched and her body naturally came better into his care.

"Oh, oh, I'm so close." Urgency rode that whisper, and she tightened her hold on his hand, pressing it closer to her body.

"Patience." Montague kissed her, showed her with his tongue exactly what he would do to her body in mere seconds, and he put every ounce of feeling into that one meeting of mouths.

When Adriana shattered, it was one of his most favorite things. She was glorious when she fell into release. The way her cheeks and chest flushed, the strangled sound of her scream that echoed in his ears, the trembling of her thighs as she rode the crest of the wave carrying her away.

Quickly, he worked the buttons of his frontfalls as his engorged length pulsed. The moment his shaft sprang forth, he repositioned himself between her legs on the leather sofa, and as she gazed at him with passion-clouded eyes, he speared into her shivering warmth, not stopping until he'd penetrated her fully.

Their groans blended together. "You are amazing," he whispered and claimed her lips, pausing for the sheer enjoyment of becoming one with her. In her he had found the healing he'd denied himself for years, and he hoped she had discovered the same with him.

"And you are a wonderfully dear man." She slid a hand down his back and when she reached an arse cheek, she squeezed. Wild sensation streaked through him. He nearly shot his wad right then. "Never could I have been forced into taking a better husband."

"That damned Lyon's Den." But the grouse had long ago lost its sting. If it hadn't been for that gaming hell, he would never have met

Adriana, and that was a depressing thought.

Then there was no need for words as he began moving within her. They waltzed together in a dance as old as time, and as she wrapped her legs about his waist, he went ever deeper each time he thrust. She canted her hips which joined them more firmly together. Deeper, faster, more frantic he pumped, drove into her with all the need and desire he had within him. Sweat plastered his shirt to his back; her soft cries of encouragement spurred him onward.

All too soon, her body stiffened. Adriana threw back her head and screamed out her pleasure in a keening cry that would no doubt have the butler investigating… after a decent few minutes of course. The fluttering contractions in her core pulled him over the edge into bliss with her, and he fell down, down, down through the rushing waves of glittering lights and infinite pleasure.

As his length jerked and pulsed, he wondered if the babe could feel what its parents had just done and whether or not it was soothing to its extremely young self. But then he collapsed into his wife's soft body fragrant of lilacs, and he sighed. Never would he tire of being here with her or reveling in what they'd found together. Always would he remain grateful.

Especially now.

"Never doubt that I love you, that I wouldn't be the man I am now without you," he whispered against the shell of her ear.

"Only if you will never doubt that I love you more." She kissed his lips, his cheek, his chin. "You make me better, and together, we will make certain London takes notice."

For a few seconds, he held her close then he slid down and off her body. When she protested, he grinned and pressed his lips to her belly, framed that soft swell with his palms. "I cannot wait until the babe grows enough so we can see that evidence." He found her gaze with his. "But even if there wasn't the possibility of this child, I would still think you were amazing. Have I not spent the past four years showing you that?"

"Oh, Montague. Yes of course." She stroked her fingers through his hair. "We have been extremely fortunate."

"Yes, we have." He had everything he'd ever wanted in his life, and that contentment was constantly surprising.

He was such a different man, he could hardly recognize himself. All thanks to the manipulation of Mrs. Dove-Lyon and her gaming hell, a place he had never stepped foot into ever since the night he and Adriana stopped hiding and were honest with each other.

And never would he let that woman know how grateful he was to her, for there was no sense in giving her additional power over him, or inflating her ego more than it was. Some things in life should remain a mystery, after all.

That secret he would keep between him and Adriana.

Nothing else mattered.

The End

About the Author

Sandra Sookoo is a *USA Today* bestselling author who firmly believes every person deserves acceptance and a happy ending. Most days you can find her creating scandal and mischief in the Regency-era, serendipity and happenstance in Victorian America or snarky, sweet humor in the contemporary world. Most recently she's moved into infusing her books with mystery and intrigue. Reading is a lot like eating fine chocolates—you can't just have one. Good thing books don't have calories!

When she's not wearing out computer keyboards, Sandra spends time with her real-life Prince Charming in central Indiana where she's been known to goof off and make moments count because the key to life is laughter. A Disney fan since the age of ten, when her soul gets bogged down and her imagination flags, a trip to Walt Disney World is in order. Nothing fuels her dreams more than the land of eternal happy endings, hope and love stories.

Stay in Touch

Sign up for Sandra's bi-monthly newsletter and you'll be given exclusive excerpts, cover reveals before the general public as well as opportunities to enter contests you won't find anywhere else.

Just send an email to sandrasookoo@yahoo.com with SUBSCRIBE in the subject line.

Or follow/friend her on social media:
Facebook: facebook.com/sandra.sookoo
Facebook Author Page: facebook.com/sandrasookooauthor
Pinterest: pinterest.com/sandrasookoo
Instagram: instagram.com/sandrasookoo
BookBub Page: bookbub.com/authors/sandra-sookoo